HER DIRTY SOLDIERS

A REVERSE HAREM ROMANCE

MIKA LANE

HEADLANDS PUBLISHING

COPYRIGHT

BE THE FIRST TO KNOW...

Want more heat, heart,
and bad boys who know what they're doing?
Join my list and I'll send the steam straight to your inbox,
starting with a deliciously naughty story:

SIGN UP TO MY MAILING LIST!
Or visit:
https://geni.us/free-book-signup

JOSS PEYTON

"Could you have been any louder last night?"

With a half-smile and shimmy of her shoulders, Sunday tossed her perfectly tousled, just-fucked hair enough to let me know she was *sorry-not-sorry* and returned to her bedroom with a cup of the expensive coffee I supplied our little household.

I knew she wasn't going to be sorry, and that was fine. I understood. A girl needed what a girl needed. But I was still compelled to let her know, as I always did, that her late-night moans and screams of *fuck me harder* did not a good roommate make.

I craned my neck from the kitchen counter toward her

room where she climbed back into bed with her coffee. Whoever the lucky guy had been, he was now gone.

Which was surprising because I was an early riser. But it was probably best to do the walk of shame before morning light. Given the chance.

Not that I had done anything like that. Recently.

"Where is he?" I called. "Did you mate and then kill?"

She dropped her head back and laughed. "You are so funny."

With my own coffee cup cleaned and in the drying rack, I reached into the hall closet and grabbed my red umbrella and the rain slicker my mother had given me. Time to tackle the bus, my glamorous journey to work.

"I'm off, Sunday. Catch ya later."

"Bye," she said dreamily, sipping my coffee.

It was going to be a long day, and not just because I hadn't gotten enough sleep the night before. Because rain was threatening, and the usual Washington, DC humidity had come early, the overheated bus was wet as a sauna. And thanks to my waterproof slicker, I was dripping with boob sweat by the time I arrived at the Georgetown Public Library.

My place of employment.

But all was not lost.

In spite of a rough morning, my spirits lifted in a surge when I ran up the steps to the stately old brick building with tall white columns. It was hands-down one of the most beautiful places I'd ever seen, which always made coming to work a little more bearable.

Not so much when I saw my boss, Candice, however.

"Morning," I called, peeling the slicker off my damp skin.

Candice poked her head around the corner, put a hand on her hip, and looked me up and down like she always did. Rumor had it she was extra-bitchy to the younger women on the library staff because she thought she was past her prime at only thirty-something years old, and was jealous of us.

I think she was just plain mean.

"You're here early," she sniffed.

I was always there early. And she always pointed it out. I don't think she knew how to start a conversation any other way.

"Yup. I was awake, so I figured I'd come in and get going on checking in that new shipment of books that came in yesterday. I'm sure the patrons will be psyched about them."

For whatever reason, we had a large contingent of readers who devoured political mysteries. Guess that sort of thing came hand-in-hand with being in a place like DC.

Candice raised a finger. "Before you do that, Joss, you're going to have to wipe down the tables and chairs. The janitor was a no-show again."

I forced my best fake-smile. It was no secret that as the lowest person on the totem pole at the library, any and all shit work landed in my lap.

But just once couldn't Candice say, instead of *you're going to have to do X*, something like *would you please do X even though it's a crummy job and theoretically not really part of your responsibilities?*

I knew better than to hold my breath.

I didn't expect a position as library assistant to be glamorous, but I was getting the feeling it was only a matter of time before she had me scrubbing the toilets.

"Sure, Candice. I'll take care of that."

The library was usually cleaned at night, but it wasn't hard to see that no one had been by. The trash cans were still full from the day before, and there were sticky fingerprints and god knew what else all over everything.

I hadn't gone to college and gotten a degree in international relations so I could clean a library. But I'd looked and looked for a job after graduation, and had to take this one at the public library when my meager savings had run out. That's when I'd gotten an apartment with my new friend, Sunday, who got laid more than a porn star. Her enthusiastic sex noises aside, she was all right.

I pulled on the yellow kitchen gloves I found under the sink in the employee break room and started wiping fingerprints and other mystery goo off the library furniture.

"Hey, Joss."

I looked up to see my brother, who occasionally visited me at work. At least when he was in town, which wasn't often.

"Booker, hey. How'd you get in? We're not even open

yet. And I didn't know you were back from your last trip yet." I gave him a quick hug.

He pointed behind himself. "Door was unlocked. And I got back last night."

And like she always did when my brother was around, Candice swanned over and put a hand on his shoulder.

It was so embarrassing.

"Well, look who it is," she flirted, tilting her head coyly.

He tried to hide his grimace. Not sure she would have noticed it anyway, that's how clueless she was.

"Hey, Candice. How are ya?" he said with an uncomfortable smile.

She pushed her chest out, but when Booker took a step away, she went back to her normal posture with a scowl, her padded bra not having caught his eye to her liking. "I'm… fine, Booker. Hey, when are we getting together for that drink?"

Wow. She was impossible to discourage.

So creepy, my boss hitting on my brother, especially when she treated me with such contempt.

Did she really think my brother would go out with her? Talk about oblivious.

It drove Booker crazy that she fawned over him when she was such a bitch to me. But he played along for my sake. He knew I needed my job, underemployed as I was with my expensive college degree. I might not make much more than minimum wage, but it was better than nothing.

"Well, Candice," Booker said, "I'm gonna have to get back to you on that, okay?" He looked at his watch.

But she wasn't easily shut down. "Okay, Booker. Play hard to get if you like. But when you come to your senses, you know where to find me." She laughed deeply and sauntered back to her perch behind the front desk where she could be rude to patrons all day.

Booker sighed and lowered his voice. "Jesus. She's the worst."

"Isn't she?" I whispered.

"Anyway, I need you to keep this bag for me," he said, pulling a cross-body satchel over his head and handing it to me. "I'll come back for it tomorrow."

He thrust it at me so fast I had no choice but to catch it.

What the hell? I didn't want to lug his shit around the city.

I pushed it back at him. "Why do I have to keep this? Can't you just take it with you?"

He rolled his eyes. "Look. Just help me out, okay?"

I rolled my eyes back. It was what we did.

"I gotta go. See you tomorrow." And he took off for the door.

I sighed, holding the bag and wondering what the hell I was supposed to do with it when I remembered we needed to discuss what to get our mom for her birthday.

I ran toward the door, and when I got to the library front steps, Booker was revving up a motorcycle and then took off speeding down the street.

The funny thing was Booker didn't ride motorcycles.

Λ

2

JOSS PEYTON

WHEN I GOT UP THE NEXT MORNING, MY ROOMMATE WAS nowhere to be found, presumably because she'd taken care of her booty call urges off-premises, as I liked to say.

It was only fair that she occasionally crashed over at some guy's house and kept *his* roommate up all night. I liked my sleep, and if there was anything that could make me bitchy, it was not getting enough of it.

Well, that, and my boss harassing me about my brother.

"Joss, your brother seems like such a *nice* guy," Candice hummed as if she could conjure another appearance from him.

He *was* nice. *That's why he's not interested in you, lady.*

Yeah, I guess I was a little protective of my big brother, not that he needed me looking out for him. But after my dad died, he'd come home from the Army and paid for me to finish college. He'd even managed to keep Mom from losing her shit. Who knew what would have happened to our little family if Booker hadn't kept us together?

That's why the likes of Candice would never be sinking her claws into him—if I had anything to say about it.

And true to her style, she gestured toward a rolling cart of books waiting for shelving.

Shelving books was considered another shit job in the world of library staff, but I actually liked it. Losing myself in the stacks of our little world got me away from Candice, and besides, introduced me to more cool books than I could ever hope to read.

So, I was cheerfully wheeling the cart out from behind the front desk to start putting the books in order, when I spotted the satchel my brother had given me the day before.

Shit. I'd completely forgotten about that stupid bag and just left it tucked behind the cart overnight. I grabbed it and brought it to the break room, hanging it under my jeans jacket so I wouldn't forget it again.

Then I remembered Booker was supposed to come back and pick it up. Where the hell was he?

Making sure Candice was off talking to some library patron about our new books, I pulled my cell out of my jacket pocket and dialed Booker.

No answer.

Weird.

I called my mother.

"Hey, Mom. Just wondering if you know where Booker is."

"Oh hi, Joss. Did you forget, he's down in Guatemala. For business or something."

Um, what?

"Mom, I don't think—"

But I stopped myself. If he told her such a bullshit story, there must be a good reason. I didn't know a lot about his work but I did know he didn't like to worry our mom.

"What's that, honey?" she asked.

"Oh, nothing, Mom. Thank you for reminding me. I don't know how I forgot that. I needed to track him down to... um, discuss your birthday gift."

She laughed. "Oh, you know I don't need a birthday gift. I just want the two of you to be happy and healthy."

We ended our call, and I peered around the corner to make sure Candice was still occupied.

Returning to the break room, I took Booker's satchel down from the coat rack and checked all the external pockets. They were empty. I shook the bag, but it was light with something soft bouncing around in it. I kind of hated going through his stuff, but I was starting to really wonder why the hell he'd left it with me, rather than keep it?

And then not show up to pick it up.

I sighed and unzipped the bag. I'd been right about the contents—all it held was a sweatshirt and pair of gym shorts.

Had he been on his way to a workout?

And why did he need me to hold his stuff?

Further, what the hell had he been doing on that motorcycle? As far as I knew, he'd never ridden one because he swore they were too dangerous.

So bizarre.

"Joss. Joss, can you come out here, please?" Candice called.

Shit. I stuffed the gym clothes back in the bag, and while I did, a piece of paper crumpled in the bottom of it. I stuffed it in my pocket and hustled over to see what my boss wanted.

"Candice. What can I do for you?"

She gestured with her chin toward the books waiting to be reshelved.

"I'm on it, Candice," I said with my fake smile.

Her glare burned my back until I was out of sight, safely ensconced in the library's quiet history section.

I pulled the paper out of my pocket that I'd found in Booker's satchel, and as I read it, my heart thumped against my chest.

Joss –

If you're opening this, that means I haven't come back to get my bag. It also means my life is likely in danger. Call the three men listed here, and tell them 'Follow the White Rabbit.'

Tell no one about this, keep the bag close, and be careful.

My friends Arrow, Cruz, and Thorn will tell you what to do next...

What the fuck?

I slumped against the bookshelves for balance because my head had started to spin and I was afraid I might lose my morning coffee.

Holy shit. What was going on?

I knew that after the Army my brother had taken a job in what he called 'private security.' He never said much about it, but he had shared that he worked for some firm that sent him on faraway trips to protect important people and stuff like that. He said he couldn't really talk about it much more than he had, and I had to admit I'd never really been interested.

And he was clearly pushing a BS 'business travel' story with our mother. It made no sense.

Now his freaking life was in danger? And I was supposed to be keeper of his cross-body bag?

It made no sense. The bag had nothing in it except for his gym clothes and the note.

But I wasn't about to ignore his instructions. I peeked around the corner and saw Candice walking an elderly lady toward the gardening books. I shot across the library, behind the front desk, and to the break room where I'd left the bag. I had no idea what was so special about it, but I wasn't going to leave it out for just anyone to see. I stuffed it into the back of one of the kitchen cabinets, behind the packets of oatmeal no one ever ate, and got back to my reshelving.

Something felt different, though.

Every person who walked in the library's front door now caught my attention. While most of them were familiar neighborhood patrons, there were a few strangers who set my imagination on fire.

Was someone trying to hurt my brother? Or me? What did he mean by telling me to 'be careful'?

Where was he and why hadn't he come back for his bag?

And who were these men I was supposed to contact?

3

ARROW SULLIVAN

Fuck *off*.

I hated solicitation calls to my cell phone.

I rolled over in bed, the room still dark, and grabbed my phone. The call was coming from a strange number. A Washington DC number. Area code two-zero-two.

Classic. The scammers make you think they're calling from someplace important.

And it was fucking six a.m.

I rolled back over in bed, and realized my um… friend from the night before was still there, snoozing lightly, her long blonde hair fanned out across the pillow on the side of the bed where I usually slept.

I never gave up my side of the bed. But this woman had conked out, and I didn't want to wake her. It would have led to another round.

And I just couldn't do it.

Not that I'd tell anyone that.

But this woman and I had fucked so much for so long, that I was actually sore, and I knew that if I were sore, she definitely was.

And that never happened to me.

The phone buzzed again.

For Christ's sake.

Same goddamn number.

And my bedmate stirred.

Shit. I didn't want her waking up before I'd slunk out of bed. Why did I have the phone switch from 'silent' to 'vibrate' at six a.m.? It's not like I was ever up at that hour.

I needed to change that shit.

The blonde sat up in bed, pushing stray pieces of hair out of her face, her small, perky tits bouncing just so.

She really was lovely. And great in the sack. It was too bad I'd never see her again. At least not on purpose.

Sure, I might run into her on the street, at happy hour, or over the summer in the Hamptons or something.

But I wouldn't be taking her out again.

There were just too many beautiful women in New York to date one of them more than once.

Yeah, I was a man whore that way. New York was full of them.

It was also full of beautiful women who said the same thing about us guys. So, I didn't feel too badly about it. I'd settle down when the time was right, I supposed. It was just that I was blowing off some much-needed steam after several years of risking my life working in private security.

"What time is it?" The blonde yawned.

I popped out of bed and pulled on my boxers. "Early, baby. Too early to be up."

My words might have bemoaned the hour, but my actions *said time to go.*

She seemed to take the hint because she wandered off to the bathroom, her beautiful upside-down heart of an ass swinging just the right amount as she walked.

I bent to pick up a sheer lace thong from my bedroom floor and quickly stuffed it in my nightstand. She wouldn't miss it.

My phone buzzed yet again. Same number.

Which was weird because the solicitation calls usually waited at least until the next day before they bothered you again.

"Who the fuck is calling me so early?" I barked into my cell.

Silence.

Good. I'd scared them off.

At least I thought so, until I heard a squeak.

"Arrow?" a small voice said.

"Hello? Who is this?"

"Um, is this… Arrow Sullivan?"

The blonde came out of my bathroom, so I went to my office for some privacy, hoping she'd get dressed and leave.

"This is he, yes," I said, looking at the sunrise over the East River.

My apartment, the largest in the building, had kick ass views to both the east and the north, so I not only saw the sunrise on the rare occasion when I was up early enough, but also had a view of upper Manhattan that included the Empire State Building, one of my favorites of all the New York landmarks.

"Oh, well, um, hi. This is Joss. Joss Peyton."

I didn't know a Joss Peyton, at least not that I could remember. Shit, I hoped she wasn't some chick I'd fucked down in DC, who was now pissed I hadn't called her.

She didn't say anything else, so I did. "What can I do for you, Miss Peyton? I am starting my workday," I lied for the benefit of the blonde now heading out my door.

I blew her a kiss, and she smiled back while closing the door. She knew the score. I didn't have her number.

Shit, I didn't even know her name.

The woman on the phone cleared her throat, her voice getting a little stronger. "I, um. I'm Booker Peyton's younger sister. He asked me to call you."

Booker Peyton. Now that was a name I hadn't heard in a while.

Fucking Booker. My private ops buddy who for some goddamn reason, was still working.

Like me, he'd made enough fuck-you money as a

warrior-for-hire doing shit the US and foreign governments didn't want to. It was lucrative stuff, but after a few years, it was time for me to get out.

Not Booker, though.

In fact, because I hadn't heard from him in so long, I was sure he was deep undercover somewhere, doing something that forced him to live in the shadows during the course of his mission.

He'd reappear eventually. He always did.

But I had no idea why his sister would be calling me.

"How'd you get my name? And my number?" I asked, my throat getting dry.

This couldn't mean anything good. There was no way Booker's sister would track me down unless something was up. Something bad.

She spoke haltingly. "The... the other day, Booker dropped a bag off with me at work. He told me he'd come back for it the next day. B... but he never showed."

Damn. He'd dragged his sister into his shit?

"So, how'd you find me?"

She lowered her voice. She was scared. "Well, when he didn't show up, I went through the bag. At first, all I found were gym clothes. But there was a piece of paper in the bottom with a message for me to call you, and that you would notify Cruz and Thorn, whoever they are."

Jesus. He was calling out the big guns.

"What did you say your name was again?" I asked.

"Joss," she said shakily.

"Okay. Joss. Did the note say anything else?"

"Yeah, it did. It said, 'follow the white rabbit.' Do you know what that means?"

Holy fuck. My empty stomach churned. Yeah, I knew what that meant.

And it wasn't good.

∧

4

ARROW SULLIVAN

"Holy shit. The gang's all here," Cruz said happily over a crackling cell line.

"Jesus, Cruz, don't they have decent cell reception in Montana?" I asked.

I could hear him moving around, presumably to find a better spot. "Damn, Arrow, you fucking called me at four a.m. I was in bed. So, give me a minute to move to a place where your princess ass can hear me better."

I loved that guy.

"What about you, Thorn? You on a secure line?" I asked.

He yawned. "Of course I am, dipshit. I wrote the code

for the most secure ones money can buy. But I bet mister cowboy in Montana doesn't have a secure line."

"And why the hell should I?" he asked, the connection much clearer now. "I'm on a fucking ranch in fucking Montana. I don't need a goddamn secure line. But I do need a large animal vet, because one of my fillies is about to give birth—"

"All right, you chatterboxes," I interrupted. "Let's make this quick."

"Sure, Arrow," Cruz said. "To what do we owe the pleasure of this reunion? I don't think I've heard from either of you two losers in a year or so."

Always the smart ass...

"Guys, this is serious. I got a call from a woman named Joss Peyton. Booker Peyton's sister. He's in trouble, and he needs us. I want you both to grab the next flights to DC. I'll meet you there at the Mayflower Hotel."

There was silence, then they both started speaking at once.

"Wait a minute, I can't just drop everything—"

and,

"I got a ranch to run, for Christ's sake—"

I raised my voice. "I don't want to hear it, guys. If Booker is asking for help, you know it's gotta be bad."

A keyboard clicked in the background. "You're right. And he sure as shit saved my ass on more than one occasion. I'm looking for flights right now," Thorn said.

I waited for Cruz to say something.

"I... I don't know. I retired from that shit, Arrow. You

know I had to. I don't know about going back in. You know what happened last time."

"Guys," Thorn interrupted, "there's a flight in two hours. I'm heading to the airport now. I'll let you know when I'm wheels down, Arrow."

Cool. Thorn was on his way.

Now I just had to convince Cruz, who I knew was a harder sell. He had good reason to be.

"Whaddya say, man? You can't turn your back on Booker, Cruz. None of us can."

He groaned. "I know. I know. I'm just letting the idea sink in. I have a foreman who can maybe watch over things. But… did he really say 'follow the white rabbit'?"

"He did, Cruz. Look. I'll pay you to come. We can't do this without you."

I knew that would shame him. Not that I was about shaming people, but I had to push him out of his comfort zone.

For Booker's sake.

"You know, Arrow…" he started to say.

Here comes my lecture.

"You can be such a manipulative asshole—"

"But you'll do it, right?" I asked.

He sighed. "Yes. I'll do it. Of course, I'll do it."

I PULLED my rented SUV into the parking garage at the Mayflower Hotel, just a few blocks from the White House, and checked into the suite I'd be sharing with the guys. I had some time to kill since Cruz was coming from somewhere in bumfuck Montana, and Thorn from San Francisco, so I started making calls to my old contacts to see what they knew about Booker's situation.

A few hours later, the guys texted me they'd arrived, and I had them brought to the suite.

"This place is nice," Thorn said, wearing his usual thick glasses, ponytail, and beat-up Army jacket. He dropped his backpack onto a sofa and nodded in approval.

"Eh. It's okay," I said. "I chose it because it was convenient and had a large suite open at the last minute."

Cruz plopped down on the sofa opposite me, still wearing his cowboy boots, plunked his elbows on his knees, and laughed. "Arrow's getting soft in his old age. He's getting spoiled."

I flipped him the bird. "Don't act like you've never been in a nice hotel. You're not fooling me."

Thorn shrugged. "I don't live high on the hog since my divorce. It's just not who I am, anyway."

Which was fine. I enjoyed the finer things in life. I'd worked hard for them, and would never go back to where I'd started. If Thorn wanted to live life frugally, that was his choice.

Cruz had buried himself in ranch life to forget his past. He shoveled cow and horse shit now.

We'd all gone in different directions, but that didn't mean we didn't have each other's backs.

Thorn found the mini-bar and helped himself to a

beer. Apparently, he wasn't completely denying himself life's pleasures. "I can't believe Booker's still taking assignments. I don't get it."

I shrugged. "I think he genuinely likes the work."

I liked the work, too—for a while. But after about the tenth time I'd nearly lost my life, I cashed the hell out. I was done trying to save the world.

But not Booker.

"Wasn't his dad killed in the line of duty? That's probably what's keeping him in the game," Cruz said.

I didn't know much about how all that went down. None of us did. Booker didn't really talk about it. But it had affected him deeply, and we figured that's why he went to work for The Company, like his father had when he was a young man.

"So where are we with things?" Thorn asked. "What do we know?"

"It's not good, guys. I did some digging around among my old contacts here in town while I was waiting for you to arrive. Booker's handler turned up dead yesterday, face down in the Potomac River."

Cruz swallowed hard. "Are you serious?"

I nodded. We all knew what that meant.

There was no one—not his employer, or the government—looking for Booker. The guy had been hung out to dry.

"Holy fucking shit," Thorn mumbled, shaking his head. "He's out there somewhere, alone, then."

"Well, he's not completely alone. He's got us now."

5

JOSS PEYTON

"Who... wha... huh...?"

I'd been yanked out of a deep sleep, and as my eyes focused in my still-dark bedroom, I realized there was a man standing over my bed.

At the sound of my stammering, he clamped a hand over my mouth.

And that's when my heart leapt into my throat.

Was this how I was going to die?

My poor mother. First, her son was full-on missing in action. And now, her daughter was going to be murdered at the hands of...

Who the fuck was in my room, anyway?

Was it Sunday's booty call?

A rando break-in?

Or someone after the satchel my brother had dumped on me?

Now I was getting pissed. And pissed was good.

With all my strength, I whipped a straight arm across my body to break his grip. I wasn't going down like this.

Of course, it did nothing.

The man held a finger to his lips. Yeah, like I was going to take this lying down.

Actually, I was lying down.

"Joss," he whispered.

What the fuck? He knew my name? And now that my eyes were adjusting to the light in my dark room, I saw he wasn't alone.

There were two others.

Three men standing over my bed. I was a goner.

"We're friends of your brother, Booker's," the one with heavy glasses said.

Friends of my brother's, my ass. They probably just wanted whatever the satchel had in it. And then they'd kill me.

But maybe it would be better if they killed me and saved my brother. At least then, my mother would lose only one kid. I always suspected she liked Booker more, anyway.

I thrashed in the direction of the man restraining me and got a good kick to his nads.

He hadn't been expecting that.

As he bent and grabbed his crotch, the other two guys grabbed my arms and legs.

Dammit.

He got his breath back after a moment. "Calm down, Joss. I'm Arrow, the guy you called in New York. We're all friends of your brother's from The Company. We're here to help."

I narrowed my eyes at him since I couldn't speak. Or move.

"I'm serious, Joss. And these are Cruz and Thorn, the other guys your brother needs help from. We were all soldiers together at one time."

I looked at them one by one. Arrow, the one with sore balls and his hand over my mouth, was clean cut and preppy like he'd just walked out of some fancy barbershop. The guy he'd called Thorn was sort of nerdy-professorial with heavy black-framed glasses and a ponytail. The other one, Cruz, was tan and rugged with hair full of sun streaks and tattoos peeking out of the sleeves of his plaid flannel shirt.

Interesting trio. I never would have put them together.

Arrow loosened his hold on my mouth. "Can we release you now? Do you promise not to scream?"

I nodded as best I could under their hold, and they slowly removed their hands. As soon as I was free, I scrambled up in bed, pulling my comforter to my chin. And as the morning light got a little brighter, I could see that the three of them were quite handsome, not to mention big, strong, and even a little mean looking.

Why hadn't Booker ever told me he had such good-looking colleagues?

"Where's my roommate?" I whispered. "And how did you get into my goddamn apartment?"

Arrow with the perfect hair looked at the tanned guy and shrugged. "No one is in the other bedroom. And… you don't need to know how we got in."

Just everyday breaking and entering skills, I supposed.

"Do you know where your roommate is, Joss?" the one with the glasses asked.

What was his name again? Thorn?

"Probably out at some booty call. She sleeps with a lot of guys."

Amusement crossed their faces, and I immediately wished I could take back my words. I hadn't meant to out Sunday. It was just a fact. She had a strong libido and was proud of it.

No judgment from me.

"Okay. We're here alone," Arrow said, helping himself to a seat on the edge of my bed.

"Where are you guys from?" I asked.

He sighed, like I should have known all that. "I'm the one you called. I live in New York. Thorn flew in from San Francisco where he's a cybersecurity expert"—he pointed at the bespectacled guy, and then the rugged one —"Cruz flew in from Montana. He has a ranch there."

"You guys came all this way for my brother?"

They nodded.

"But why? Do you think he's... in some kind of trouble?"

They looked at each other before speaking, then Cruz started. "Your brother... is pretty much a hero in our eyes, and we'd do anything to help him. In fact, he saved my life on more than one occasion. And yes, we think he could be in... trouble."

What?

"Um, I knew my brother did something with security. But are you saying it was a dangerous job? Like, really dangerous?"

Cruz nodded slowly.

"So... what does that mean, exactly?" I asked, my voice choking. "I mean, how bad could it really be? Right?"

I looked from one to the other.

Blank faces all around.

Finally, Arrow spoke. "He wouldn't have had you call us if things weren't serious."

I put my head in my hands. I didn't know who these guys were, and what did they know, anyway?

Booker would never get himself into a bad situation. He was too smart for that.

They were being dramatic. Everything would be fine.

I jumped out of bed, which I should have thought twice about, because there I stood in the undies and a tank top that I always slept in. But I didn't have time to be embarrassed. Or modest.

I wanted to know what the hell was going on with my brother.

I ran to my dresser and pulled on jeans and a T-shirt.

"You all don't have to stare, you know," I griped, and they quickly looked down. Well, except for the guy with the glasses.

Guess he didn't see half-naked women too often.

"Joss, you told me your brother gave you a bag," Arrow said.

Shit. Why did I tell him that? I needed to keep some of these things closer to my vest until I had some confidence in these guys. Sure, Booker had asked me to contact them, but couldn't they go do their own thing and let me do mine?

I pulled on my Converse Chucks, stood to my full height, and put my hands on my hips. "Yes, I have the bag. It's someplace safe."

Silence. I liked people who could read between the lines. These guys were clearly no dummies.

They were going to have to accept that I was in charge, and not the other way around.

But instead of acknowledging my clear authority, Arrow jumped to his feet and made his way to my bedroom door, with Cruz and Thorn close behind.

What the hell?

"Sounds like you've got it under control, Joss," Cruz said as they all made their way to my front door. "We'll let you get to it, then."

Wait. They were leaving?

"Nice meeting you," Thorn called over his shoulder.

Arrow waved from the open door. "Good luck with your brother."

And they were gone.

Okay. I could handle this.

Or not.

∧

6

JOSS PEYTON

"Wait!" I screamed, running after them.

They stopped and turned in my building's hallway, their faces covered in amusement.

I waved them back. "Please," I begged.

Jerks, calling my bluff like that.

But my pride didn't matter. My brother's face flashed before my eyes.

Yeah, I could look for him, but maybe his buddies from their private security world knew a thing or two about finding people.

I mean, they'd all come from out of town and had gone through the trouble of breaking into my apartment. And scaring the shit out of me.

As soon as they were back inside, I led them to our tiny kitchen, where they sat in the breakfast nook.

"Coffee?" I asked.

They nodded.

Thorn raised a finger. "Oh hey, do you have chai tea, or something like that? Preferably organic?"

The other guys gave him such dirty looks, he put his finger back down.

While the coffee was brewing, I fetched the bag from my room where I'd hidden it, brought it to the kitchen, and plopped it down on the table.

"Here you go."

They stared at it for a moment, I suppose looking for something that might have gone right over my head, and Arrow reached for it. He went through every outer pocket, just like I had, then opened it and turned it inside out.

Thorn picked up the sweatshirt and shorts that tumbled to the floor, shaking them out and running his fingers over every seam.

What was he hoping to find?

Arrow passed the bag to Cruz for his inspection. "Where's the note, Joss?"

I reached into my back pocket, and laid it on the table.

Thorn unfolded the note so they could all see it. "Does this look like your brother's handwriting?"

I nodded. "Yeah. That's totally his chicken scratch. Tell me, what in the world does 'follow the white rabbit' mean?"

They glanced at each other, and Thorn spoke slowly as he powered up the laptop he'd pulled out of his backpack. "It's an old Company term. It indicates a big… problem."

No shit. I could have told them that. But if they wanted to be a bunch of snotty secret-keepers, that was on them.

"Do you need my network password?" I offered, trying to be helpful.

He looked at me like I'd just asked the stupidest thing ever.

Okay. 'Helpful me' was about done with this group.

Cruz waved in my direction. "He's a cybersecurity dude. He has his own network he travels with."

"Networks," he corrected, stressing the *s*.

These guys weren't messing around.

Thorn tapped on his keyboard and turned the laptop so Arrow and Cruz could see it.

"Wow. Dude, nothing gets past you," Arrow said, nodding.

"What?" I asked, hovering, unable to see what they were looking at. "What did you find?"

Thorn turned the laptop my way, but I had no idea what I was looking at.

"Your brother used 'follow the white rabbit' as a URL to go to where he left more info."

"Okay. Well does it say where he is?" I asked.

Thorn shook his head. "No, because when he put this page together, he didn't know where he was going to be taken."

"Or *if* he was even going to be taken," Arrow added.

"Then what's on there that's helpful?" I asked.

"It's in code, but I think he's provided names and contact info of some of the people who took him."

I didn't get it. What was with all the secrecy, codes, mysterious URLs, and other crap? It just sounded like a bunch of time-wasting drama if you asked me.

I refilled everybody's coffee. "I'll be in my room. I need a moment."

They nodded thoughtfully and went back to their theorizing.

I grabbed a seat in my bedroom corner's reading chair, a nasty old piece of furniture I'd been lugging around since college.

Actually, I think it had been Booker's before mine. He was already out of the house by the time I left for college, so I took it with me, managing to cram it into every dorm room and apartment I'd lived in.

When my dad died in a car wreck, Booker left the Army and came right home. He just swooped in and took care of everything.

He couldn't make my father come back, but he damn sure tried to make up for his being gone.

A lump grew in my throat while I thought about what kind of trouble he could be in. I had to do something. And these guys—his supposed 'buddies'—were sitting at my kitchen table drinking my good coffee and flapping their gums.

I quietly grabbed the set of keys I had to Booker's

apartment, pulled on my jeans jacket, and slipped out the door without alerting the guys.

His friends could sit around on their asses all day for all I cared. I flagged down a cab and went to Booker's apartment in the Adams Morgan neighborhood. I actually could have walked the distance from my place to his in about fifteen minutes, but time was of the essence, and if Arrow, Cruz, and Thorn were heading over, I wanted to beat them there.

I'd show them they weren't the only ones with ideas.

7

CRUZ DUFRESNE

"WHAT ARE WE SUPPOSED TO DO WITH THIS? ANY thoughts, Thorn?"

Arrow jumped to his feet in frustration, pointing at the laptop with some weird-ass message Booker was trying to convey.

The guy was too smart by half. Even our resident Einstein, Thorn, didn't know what it meant.

If he couldn't figure this shit out, we were screwed.

I couldn't lie. My brains were dulled by a couple years of rounding up cattle and breaking horses on my Montana ranch. There was a gentle rhythm to the days there, which admittedly could be harsh, especially in winter, but life there soothed me. Most days were pretty much like the day before, and while that might sound dull to some, it had saved my life.

A major bonus was that I pretty much always knew I'd be alive to see the next day's sunrise—a sentiment that was a luxury back when I was in private security. I got paid a fuck-ton of money to do what I did back then, but the toll it took was deadly—literally and figuratively.

It was the biological and psychological price of being the kind of soldiers we were.

Even though I'd been trained as a doctor. That had served me for a while. Until it didn't. I saw too much death in the field to be able to face it any longer

But the old instincts were coming back, the thought processes of being on a mission. And if I were honest, I had to say it felt kind of good.

"I guess we start at his apartment, then," Thorn said, jerking me back to the conversation.

Arrow craned his neck in the direction of Joss's room. "Is she all right? She hasn't made a peep since she left us," he said quietly.

Now, Thorn and I peered that way too, but couldn't see much from the kitchen. "Do you think she went back to bed?"

Something felt off. Very off.

I jumped out of my chair so fast it fell back with a *bang*, and in three long steps was in Joss's room, where the day had started.

It was empty.

Fuck all.

"Guys. She's gone."

"ARROW, are you trying to kill us?"

I held tight to the 'oh shit' handle while he sped across DC, blowing through more than one red light. This was not how I wanted to die.

"I'm fucking pissed, Cruz. She should have known not to take off by herself."

I tightened my grip as Arrow careened around another corner. "I think she did know she shouldn't take off, and that's why she sneaked out."

"Do you think she's on the up and up? I mean, what if she's setting us up?" Thorn said.

The car's *Waze* app could barely keep up with how fast Arrow was driving.

"I think she's legit," he said. "It just doesn't seem like Booker's sister could be working for the other side."

Booker's sister. I never even knew he had one. He just didn't talk about his family, aside from the death of his father.

The commonly understood story was that Will Peyton was in an automobile accident traveling for business on the island of Malta. But those of us with The Company knew the real story. Peyton had been closing in on a Russian counterspy. The spy's people got to Peyton before he could be removed from the situation. One of the saddest things was that it was to have been his last job. The man was a week away from retiring.

Shortly after that, Booker was discharged from the Army and came to work with us, following in his father's footsteps. I think the fact that he was still taking missions, rather than retiring like the rest of us, spoke to his anger over his father's death, and some sort of endless drive for revenge.

But if he had retired, we'd never have met his sister. What a beauty she turned out to be. No wonder he'd never mentioned her.

Joss wasn't beautiful in the classic sense, but in a different sort of way, with her swingy chin-length hair, full lips, and slightly crooked nose—probably the result of a childhood tussle with her older brother. She had that urban-hipster thing going on. You didn't see much of that in Montana.

And the ass on her. I knew we were working a case, but when a woman leaps out of bed in a pair of panties and a skimpy tank top, well, the old libido wakes up pretty quickly.

Just like my dick did.

And I felt bad about that. The woman's brother, who was also my friend, was in danger—possibly mortal danger—and I was thinking about the way the cheeks of her ass jiggled as she stormed around her bedroom, getting dressed in front of all us guys.

I had to hand it to her. The woman was gutsy.

"Christ, I hope she's not as crazy as her brother," Thorn said.

Arrow laughed. "Don't count on it. I'm getting the feeling it runs in the family."

"You know, this feels good, guys," I said.

Thorn tapped on the dashboard while we were stuck at a light. "What feels good, Cruz? Risking our life in a vehicle driven by Arrow?"

Shit, I'd been in worse. We all had.

"Good one, Thorn. No, what I mean is that I feel like I'm doing something good by helping our old buddy Booker. Hell, I owe that guy my life."

I actually owed him for several heroic actions, but the one I remembered best was a mission—I couldn't remember where—and I was the team doctor. I had it easy, I'll admit it. I didn't have to tussle with any of the bad guys or get shot at or any dangerous shit like that. I mostly just lurked in the background and if any of the guys got blown, I was there to try to put them back together.

All that changed the day our convoy was ambushed. Everyone in my vehicle was injured, including myself. There was a fire, and Booker could only rescue one of us.

The one he rescued?

Let's just say it was my lucky day.

So, yeah. If the guy needed something, I was going to be there for him no matter what.

Arrow slapped his hand on the steering wheel as Booker's address came into view. "Guys, I am here for our friend. Not his sister. If she's going to run off and do stupid things, that's her problem. We can't save both their asses."

He had a point. And I wasn't sure I liked it all that much.

"For Christ's sake, Arrow, don't you think Booker would want us to protect his sister just as much as he wants our help, if not more so? He's a massively unselfish guy, and I'd bet money that if it were down to his life or hers, he'd say to save her first," I said.

Arrow pulled over to the side of the street, just across from Booker's apartment building. Christ, I didn't know he lived in such a happening neighborhood, with restaurants, bars, and tons of people on foot.

The perfect place to blend in. Not be noticed. Smart.

Made me feel like I'd been holed up in Montana for too long. I hadn't realized how I missed the buzz of the city.

Arrow scanned the area before hopping out of the SUV. "I don't know. I maintain our job is to save Booker and no one else. But I see your point."

"Hey. Do you guys see those couple cars over there? The ones where the guys in the driver's seat are reading the paper?"

Thorn laughed. "Christ, do people still use that as a cover? Like are they unaware that people do most of their reading on their devices these days?"

"Speak for yourself. I still like actual books and newspapers," I said.

Thorn turned around in the front seat. "Well shit, bro, you're in fucking Montana. Do you even have electricity there?" He dropped his head back and laughed his ass off.

They loved giving me shit about bailing on civilization. All I could say was, wait till they tried it, if they ever did. They'd never go back.

"Yeah, they're definitely staking out the place. What a couple of idiots. They're not even looking at the paper," Arrow said.

"Don't judge a book by its cover. They may be lousy at stake outs, but I bet they're lethal as hell," Thorn said, sinking down in his seat and snapping photos of the guys.

"Do you think Joss is here? I mean, where else would she start, if not her brother's apartment," he added.

Arrow nodded. "Yeah. I bet she's inside right now. She is not answering her phone. I wish we'd had time to put a tracker in it. Damn."

"Seriously. If she hadn't taken off so fast, I could have totally done it," Thorn said.

Arrow watched some of the pedestrians. "I will say, boys, that it's quite possible that the women in DC are even better looking than those in New York. They're a bit more buttoned up with their suits and shit, but they sure are pretty."

"Dude, you're such a horn dog that even on a mission you're thinking of getting laid," Thorn said, punching Arrow in the shoulder.

His eyebrows rose. "Oh really? You're telling me you didn't take a good long look at Booker's hot little sister this morning when she was walking around in her underwear?"

Busted, Thorn looked out his passenger side window. "Yeah, I looked. And yeah, she's hot. In a kind of slightly nerdy way. Which happens to be the way I like it."

All ribbing aside, it was good to hear Thorn talking about women. He'd been so devastated by his divorce we were afraid he'd never try to date again.

"Well, I guess a nerd knows a nerd. Know what I mean?" I said.

"You're damn right, asshole," he said. "And it's served me quite well."

He wasn't kidding. He was one of the foremost cyber-security experts in the country. Actually, probably the world.

"Hey, guys. Is that Joss over there?"

I craned my neck and saw her in front of the building, waiting by the circular drive.

"Fuck me," Arrow said, releasing his seat belt. "It's her. And she's talking to some guy who has his hand on her arm."

"Shit, check it out. The guys in the stakeout cars are suddenly looking very interested, too," I took off my own seatbelt, ready to run.

"All right, guys. The usual drill," Arrow said. "I'll come in from the left, you Thorn, from the right, and Cruz goes head on."

We jumped out of the SUV and without even looking for coming cars, made our way toward Joss. While the argument might have been about whether we were supposed to watch over her at all, the truth of the matter was that we probably couldn't find Booker without her anyway.

And that should give us ample opportunity to get to know the lovely Joss Peyton.

8

JOSS PEYTON

"Hi, Miss Peyton. Haven't seen your brother in a while."

Crap. I'd hoped to slip by the doorman in Booker's building without a conversation.

"Oh hey, Phil. Yeah, he's out of town. I'm just here to get his mail," I lied.

"He's out of town? I could swear I just saw him a couple days ago—"

Why was the distance from Booker's lobby to the elevators so long? I could never just slip into my brother's building without a conversation with someone.

I picked up my pace. "In a hurry Phil," I called over my shoulder.

"But, Miss Peyton, the mailboxes are over here," he said, pointing to a small room just behind his desk.

Well, shit.

I laughed breezily. "Right. But I gotta water his plants, first."

He smiled and got back to his computer, and I jumped into the first elevator that opened.

Fuck. At least in my building no one gave a shit whether you lived or died. I liked that kind of privacy.

Especially when I had three very hunky friends of my brother's breaking into my apartment at the crack of dawn.

Seriously. How did those guys know they wouldn't end up arrested or something? Or that I didn't have a gun?

In their world, it might be okay to enter people's homes without their permission, but it wasn't in mine.

At the same time, I was happy they'd shown up to support my brother. They'd all traveled a long way. I was grateful for their dedication toward Booker. I really was. But that didn't mean I was going to sit on my ass and do nothing just because they'd arrived.

I made it down the hallway toward my brother's apartment, a lovely condo he'd bought a couple years back, after he finished paying for my college. At the time, I'd hinted around that I wouldn't mind being his roommate, but he made it clear that was a no-go.

Guess he didn't want me to cramp his style.

So, I stayed at my mom's in the suburbs until I had a

little money saved from doing odd jobs, and when it came time to find a roommate to share with, Sunday had sort of just appeared in my life. I hardly remembered exactly how we met, actually. It felt like we'd been friends forever.

I think I'd been at happy hour with my friends and she just sort of joined the party. She told me she thought I was super cool and wanted to hang out again.

It was sort of like getting picked up, except by a girl.

Anyway, she fit into my posse without a hitch and everyone loved her. She'd insisted we look for a place together. She could probably have gotten her own—it seemed her parents were pretty well, and besides, she never really worked. With the amount of sex she had, she probably should have gotten her own apartment. But I got the feeling she just wanted company.

And I wanted someone to share expenses with, so it was a win-win.

So even though my brother wouldn't let me live with him, he still gave me a spare key and let me stay there when he was out of town. Well, until I invited some friends over and someone puked in his bedroom and didn't tell me.

After that, I wasn't allowed back for a while. But he got over it.

And now, I was fumbling with the key to his apartment. The lower lock turned easily.

Strange.

That was the one lock that always stuck.

And then I realized, it hadn't been locked at all.

Huh. Booker always used both the bottom and top lock. In fact, he was pretty fastidious about that sort of thing.

So, I slipped the key into the upper lock, the deadbolt.

It wouldn't turn.

At all.

I knocked on his door. I wasn't exactly sure why, because he wasn't in there, but it just seemed like the thing to do.

I tried the key again.

No luck.

Shit. Booker's neighbors would soon be emerging to head out to work for the day, and I didn't want to get caught up making small talk with any of them, so I scurried back to the lobby to get the hell out of there.

Speaking of work, I needed to get to my own job. Today was the one day a week the library was open late. Since I'd agreed to close up, I didn't have to be there until eleven a.m.

On my way out I paused by the front desk to talk to the doorman. "Hey, Phil, do you know if Booker changed his locks or something? I can't get into his apartment."

He furrowed his brow. "Not that I know of. When tenants do that, they usually tell us and make sure we have a copy of the new key. You know, for just in case."

Could someone else have changed his locks? Who would do that? And why?

I said my goodbyes to Phil before I alarmed him any further, and walked outside to the circular drive where a cab waited for its passenger. The morning sun felt good for a moment, but then it occurred to me I was no further along with finding my brother than I had been the day he'd not shown up for his bag. I doubted his buddies had made any progress, either. They were probably still at my apartment messing around with their laptop.

I squinted in the morning light while I thought about what to do next. Booker wasn't answering his phone and the key to his apartment wouldn't work. There must be something else I could try...

A tap on the shoulder snapped me out of my reverie.

"Hey. I know you."

I turned to face a nice-looking, typical DC dude with neatly-trimmed hair, wire-rimmed glasses, a starched dress shirt, and gray trousers.

He extended his hand for a shake. "Joss, right? We went to college together."

Huh. I normally remembered faces.

It must have been pretty obvious I was at a loss, because the guy didn't waste a moment recapping how we'd met.

He smiled. "You hung out with the folks in the seniors' dorm, right? I went to a few of the parties you guys held."

Oh. Right. It was coming back to me now. Shit. Had I slept with him?

"And what was your name?" I asked.

He seemed surprised I didn't remember.

Whatever, dude.

"Steve. Steve Mueller."

I nodded. "Right. Well good to see you again. Do you live here?" I asked, pointing behind myself.

He pushed his glasses up. "Oh no, just here to visit a friend. You?"

He was visiting a friend at eight a.m.?

"My brother lives here. I was just… checking his mail. He's… traveling."

He looked around, like he was waiting for something. "You're a nice sister."

A car pulled up in the drive and stopped in front of us.

He pulled the backseat door open. "Here's my Uber. I gotta run now—"

"I thought you were here to visit someone—" I started to say.

And the next thing I knew, he had an iron grip on my upper arm, and was shoving me toward the car.

"Hey!" I screamed. "Get the fuck off me!"

With my free arm, I punched him right in the eye, bending the frame of his glasses and popping out the lens. I knew I wouldn't be able to hit very hard, but if I smashed his glasses into his face, I had a chance.

One of the advantages of growing up with a brother was learning how to fight.

And my plan worked. He released me and his hands flew up to his face. He yanked off the glasses and glared.

"You bitch—" he growled, and came for me again.

Okay, I was pretty sure I didn't know this guy from college.

Just then I heard my name yelled.

"Joss, get inside!"

It was Cruz, sprinting across the building's front lawn.

The guy with the glasses reached for me one more time, but I was too fast. I ran, and with a backward glance saw Cruz, Arrow, and Thorn closing in on my would-be captor. But he jumped into the backseat of the car before they reached him, and the driver took off screeching down the driveway and into the morning rush hour traffic.

"Miss Peyton. You okay?" Phil asked, surprised at my return to the lobby.

He came out from behind his desk and put a kind hand on my shoulder. He missed the whole thing, thankfully. I didn't need him alerted to my shit show.

"I… yes, I just… forgot to check Booker's mail," I lied, rubbing my arm where I'd been grabbed.

The lobby doors opened, and Cruz casually sauntered in, smiling. "Oh, here you are, baby. Ready to head out?"

Huh?

He slung an arm around my shoulders. "Joss, you don't want to be late for work, do you?"

I looked up at him and he widened his eyes.

Oh.

I got it.

"You're right, honey," I said, shaking my head. "I'll get Booker's mail next time. See ya, Phil."

But before we reached the door, Cruz stopped. He raised his hand to stroke the stubble on his chin.

"Excuse me," he said, addressing Phil, "you don't happen to have security cameras, do you?"

Phil's face got serious. "Actually, we do. But they went out of order just a couple days ago. It's the strangest thing. I've been here for years, and we've never had any trouble. Someone came by to perform maintenance on the system, and poof, they stopped working. Ya know, it's so hard to get competent workers these days…"

My stomach acid churned, and I was getting warm. Like really warm.

Whoever had taken Booker had been here, and made sure there was no record of their visit.

Or my near my abduction.

Cruz, sensing my distress, tightened his hold on my shoulders. "Interesting. Well then, have a good day."

He steered me toward the door, but Phil stopped us.

"Sir, were you wanting to look at the security tapes? Did something happen that I need to know about?"

Cruz laughed. "Oh, no, man. Didn't mean to alarm you. My own apartment building is talking about installing cameras, so I was just curious."

Relaxing, Phil waved goodbye. "I'll see ya later, Miss Peyton. And if I see your brother, I'll ask him about the lock situation. We need to take care of that."

"Thanks, Phil," I called over my shoulder.

Arrow and Thorn stood at the end of the driveway, where they started peppering me with questions.

"Where the hell did you go?"

"Are you fucking crazy?"

"Do you never want to see your brother again?"

"Shut up!" I snapped. "Jesus. A girl can't think. Your questions feel like a… firing squad or something."

As they looked at me, surprised at my outburst, my bravado crumpled, and like a broken faucet, the waterworks started. Mortified, I buried my face in my hands.

"Are you okay?" Cruz asked.

I shook my head, *no*. "What do we do now? Who's going to save my brother?"

Arrow hooked a finger under my chin and turned my face up to look at him.

I was sure I was a vision, all red-eyed and snotty.

"What the hell do you think we came to town for? To meet you?"

9

JOSS PEYTON

THE GUYS PACKED ME INTO AN SUV, AND ARROW TOOK THE
wheel, turning in the direction of the White House.

"Where are we going?" I bawled.

How did I know these guys were on the right side?

How did I know *anything*?

"You've been compromised. Now that they know who
you are, you can't go back home," he said.

"What?" I cried.

"We'll get you a room adjoining ours at the Mayflower.
It's the only way we can keep you safe," Thorn said,
tapping on his laptop.

Safe?

"What do you mean?" I asked.

He looked over his shoulder at me. "Whoever tried to grab you just now, they aren't giving up and just walking away. They'll try again, Joss. We can't just let you go home and pretend everything is fine."

"Are we all set?" Arrow asked, glancing at Thorn.

"Almost," Thorn said, tapping a few more keys. "There we go. Got it."

I didn't know what these guys were about, but I was not going to any hotel. I needed to get home, cleaned up, and get to work by eleven a.m. My brother might be in danger, and maybe on some level I was too, but I still needed to get to work. I'd just be… careful where I went and who I talked to.

That's all I needed to do.

Right?

"Guys, please just take me home, okay? I appreciate your concern, but—"

"Bingo!" Thorn interrupted. "Got it."

"What? What did you get?"

Cruz patted my hand. "Thorn just broke into the hotel's reservation system and booked you into the room attached to our suite."

I looked at him, then Thorn up front. "Why? I'm not going to the hotel with you. I just told you."

He looked out the window cockily. "Man, the Mayflower's cybersecurity sucks. I hacked that in a matter of minutes."

I was glad he impressed himself, because he hadn't impressed me.

And Arrow just kept driving *away* from the direction of my apartment, like he hadn't heard me.

"Thanks for the five-star invite, guys, but I have to get to work. So please, Arrow, turn this car around and head for my apartment. You know, the one you broke into this morning?"

Cruz spoke patiently. "Joss, you can't go home. Your life is in danger."

"Bullshit! I have things to do. I have a life," I insisted. "I don't get to just disappear to a fancy hotel and hole up like you guys do. I have responsibility. Commitments I've made."

Thorn spoke over his shoulder. "That's right, you have a life. Today. But if you don't do what we tell you, you won't have that life much longer."

Holy shit. What sort of mess did Booker get me into?

I swear, when he resurfaced, we were going to have a serious come-to-Jesus talk. I did not need this kind of crap in my life.

I sat back in my seat, arms crossed, and looked out my window at all the Washingtonians rushing to work. "But I need stuff. Stuff from my apartment."

Arrow glanced at me in the rear-view. "Okay. We can swing by your place. But you have ten minutes. Thorn will go up with you and pretend to be your… friend or something. In case you run into your roommate or anybody else."

Wow. Ten whole minutes to shove my life into a bag.

I wiped away a tear. I wasn't usually one for crying,

but fuck all. I felt like life as I knew it was over, and coupled with my fears of not seeing my brother again, I was pretty close to being wrecked.

Cruz took a deep breath. "I know this is a lot, Joss. But your brother needs us, and now that you're in danger, he'd want us to protect you, too. Can you imagine if we freed him, only to find out something had happened to you? How do you think that would make him feel?"

Okay. The old guilt trip. Worked every time.

We pulled up in front of my building, and Thorn opened my door. He took my hand when I stepped out of the SUV, and while we walked up the steps to my building, he didn't let go.

10

THORN JENSEN

"Damn. They didn't take long, did they?"

I followed Joss's horrified gaze around her apartment —the nice and tidy little home we'd been drinking coffee in just one hour earlier.

Unfortunately, her place was no longer nice *or* tidy. In the small amount of time it had taken for her to run over to her brother's, nearly be kidnapped, and dragged back here by us, someone had ransacked the place. From where I stood, it appeared her bedroom was hit the hardest, followed by the living room, and then her roommate's room, which had sustained little more upheaval than open dresser drawers and an upended lamp.

Whoever had searched the place seemed to know what they were looking for.

"Oh my god. Were they looking for the bag?" she mumbled, righting a spilled potted plant.

"Stand back for a sec, Joss. Let me make sure the coast is clear first," I whispered.

But a quick tour indicated that whoever had broken in had done their damage and hit the road.

"Two break-ins in one day. First you guys, and now this. I'd always thought this apartment was safe," she said flatly.

I felt for her. What she was going through was no fun.

"If it makes you feel any better, Joss, your apartment probably is really safe. It's just that no lock can stand up to guys like Arrow, Cruz, or me. Or the folks who broke in. We have… talents the average person knows nothing about."

She glared at me. "Well, good for you."

Stepping over the debris littering her floor, I put my hands on her shoulders and directed her toward her bedroom. "Let's get going, Joss. Remember, Arrow said ten minutes. He wasn't kidding. If we're not down at the car by then, he will come up and carry you down. And you won't have any of your stuff."

She sighed loudly and reached under her bed to retrieve a giant duffel bag, which she began maniacally cramming things into. I guess it was easier to pack when your shit was all over the place like it was, thanks to whomever had broken in, but I wasn't sure she was even looking at what she was throwing in the bag. It was like she was on one of those game shows where you raced to fill up a shopping cart, and got to keep whatever you managed to fit in it.

"Can I help with anything, Joss? Don't forget your… you know, shampoo and stuff, if that's the sort of thing you like to bring with you."

She looked at me and nodded, darting into the kitchen for a plastic bag and then disappearing into the bathroom. Seconds later, she flew out, the bag now packed with god-knew-what, and paused to look around.

"Oh wait. Let me get my Kindle. And dammit, where is my sketch pad?" she murmured, looking around in a panic.

I knew she had an artsy bent. I was a goner now.

She was already rocking the sexy librarian look, and what was even hotter was that she seemed to have no freaking idea. Her dark, chin-length hair, whipping around her face with every movement, was a sharp contrast to her pale, never-been-in-the-sun complexion. The only makeup she seemed to wear was a bright red lipstick on her full mouth. That, coupled with her tight jeans and cropped T-shirt, seriously got my motor revving.

She was definitely my type.

Funny thing was, I think she was Arrow's and Cruz's type, too.

"I... I have to just leave my apartment a mess like this? My roommate will flip."

I heaved her duffel over my shoulder and let her take one last look around. "Yeah, she probably will. But she'd freak out even worse if she came home and found you dead."

Joss looked like she might throw up.

I needed to be more careful with how I spoke to civilians.

She pulled her apartment door closed behind us, ironically securing both the top and bottom locks, which clearly had not kept out the day's intruders—myself included. But it was probably a ritual that felt good and provided a modicum of control in a fucked-up situation.

We jogged down the stairs and reached the SUV just as Arrow was getting out.

"Here you are. I was beginning to wonder if you guys stopped for lunch or something," he laughed.

I wanted to tell him it wasn't the best time to make jokes, but I wasn't getting into it in front of Joss. If he wanted to stick his foot in his big mouth, he could go right ahead.

Joss leaned her head against the cool glass of her window and closed her eyes as Arrow pulled into traffic.

"Well guys, someone had already ransacked the place. It was pretty trashed," I said.

"Shit," Cruz mumbled, shaking his head. "That didn't take long."

He wasn't surprised. None of us were, with the exception of Joss. Raided homes came with the territory, as she was learning.

Arrow was more amused than anything. "That's fine, considering we already have what they were looking for." He chuckled as he pulled into traffic.

"What am I going to do about work today?" Joss asked quietly, as if she'd resigned herself to listening to us.

"You'd better call your boss, sweetie," Cruz said.

He was always so fucking nice.

"Yeah. You're right. Everyone be quiet, okay?" she said.

Arrow switched the radio off.

"Hi, Candice," Joss said in a weak voice. "I'm not feeling well. I'm afraid I won't be able to make it in today. I'm really sorry."

Unintelligible squawking filled the car, accented by Joss's responding with *mmmm-hmm* and *okay*.

It wasn't hard to tell that she was getting her ass handed to her.

What kind of boss bitches you out when you're sick?

"What was that, Candice?" Joss asked, her voice getting shrill. "Oh. Well, okay. Thanks for letting me know. Yeah, I'll talk to you later."

She ended the call.

"Wow," she said quietly, looking out the window.

As we approached the Mayflower's parking garage, both Arrow and I did a sweep of the area to ensure we weren't being followed.

Old habits died hard.

"Everything okay, Joss?" Cruz asked.

She took a moment to answer. "My boss said someone had been by the library looking for me. They asked her all sorts of questions. She assumed it was some guy who wanted to ask me out. But she said he wore crooked wire-rimmed glasses that were slightly bent."

∧

11

THORN JENSEN

"I think you'll be comfortable here, Joss."

I watched her look around her new home with skeptical appreciation. The room I'd managed to snag for her, thanks to my hotel reservation hacking skills—pretty basic in the cyber community, but I still claimed bragging rights—was far more luxe than her own apartment with its second-hand furniture and collegiate wall hangings.

I dropped her duffel off on the bed and headed for the door connecting the two rooms. I figured she'd probably like some time to get settled in, and besides, I wanted to talk to the guys about next steps, preferably out of her earshot.

Turning before I made my exit, I found her plopping

on the end of the bed, and I had to say, looking pitiful as hell.

It was understandable.

She looked back at me, resigned. "Hey, Thorn?"

"Yeah?"

"Thank you."

She wiped her eyes with the back of her sleeve and sniffled.

Crap. I had work to do, but it was no time to run out on the poor girl.

I took a seat next to her. "It sucks, I know, not being home, not going to work, not knowing where your brother is. But you have to believe you've got the right guys working on this. If there is anyone in the world who can help Booker, it's the three of us. And you seem to be pretty motivated to find him, too. The way you punched out that skinny dork was epic."

She gave me a weak smile. "I appreciate it. And it felt good to belt that creep. Sorry for the trouble today. I just have to let you know, though, that if I don't think you're doing all you can, I'm not going to just sit there and be quiet."

I should have known she wasn't going to sit back and wait for things to happen. Just like her big brother. Bull-headedness seemed to be a Peyton trait.

"I don't blame you for feeling impatient. But please work with us on this." I placed a casual arm around her shoulder to comfort her, but she just smelled so damn good, like roses and good old fresh air. I leaned a little closer, hoping she wouldn't notice.

She hadn't. "Hey. I'm starving. Could we get something to eat?"

I was hungry too. "How about I order us something?"

She shook her head. "I need to get out. Walk around the block a couple times. It's like I'm stuffed with pins and needles and can't sit still. Can we do that? Is it possible?"

Ah. Good old anxiety. I knew it well.

"I'll tell you what. Let me run out to the store for a couple things that will work as a disguise. Then, we can get something to eat."

Her face brightened. "Really? Oh my god, that would be great. I think it's just the feeling of being hemmed in that's bumming me out. But if I know that I can go out once in a while, if I absolutely have to, that takes the pressure off."

I got it. A prisoner who wasn't a prisoner.

She could actually leave any time she wanted to. We could only pressure her to stay, but if she didn't, there was no way to force her to listen. She'd be crazy for defying our advice, but if she insisted on it, well the door was open.

We were all about personal responsibility.

Not that she knew that.

Thirty minutes later, I returned to find her watching some movie. But when she saw me, she clicked off the TV and came running over to see what I'd found.

"Oh my god, oh my god, let's see what you got," she said, bouncing up and down.

I dumped the contents of my bags, the result of visiting two different drug stores, on the bed. First, I opened the bag with a short blonde wig stuffed in it. It was more of a Halloween wig than a fashion wig, but for our purposes, it would do just fine.

In addition to that, I unwrapped a baseball cap, and some of those clear glasses people use with computers.

"Have you ever worn a wig?" I asked.

She laughed. "No. Have you?"

I wasn't going to answer that question. She'd eventually learn all she needed to know about our line of work.

"First put on this cap and tuck your hair into it really tightly."

She wrestled with the flesh-colored cap, and when her hair was completely covered, I pulled the wig down over it.

"How do I look?" she asked hopefully.

Whew. That was one cheap costume wig.

"Like a PTA mom at some kid's elementary school. All you need are those high-waisted jeans."

Her mouth dropped open she play-slapped me. "No way."

She ran to the mirror and gasped. "Holy shit. You weren't kidding."

"Yeah. I miss your dark hair." I grimaced.

Shit. Did I really just say that?

She glanced at me, then looked back in the mirror,

yanking on the sides of the wig as if that would make it longer.

"It really is kind of ugly, isn't it?" she said, laughing.

I tossed her the hat. "Hey, it's a disguise, not a fashion show."

She pulled the cap over the wig and grabbed the glasses I'd picked up.

I had to say, she did look like a different person.

I peeled off my crappy old Army jacket and held it out for her, followed by a pink lipstick I'd found in a sale bin. "C'mon. This will be the *piece de resistance*. Wipe off that red stuff you wear and try this Barbie Doll pink."

I stepped back to take her in. Wow. It would be fucking hard, if not impossible, to identify her as Joss Peyton, younger sister of Booker Peyton, hot as hell DC girl.

Λ

12

JOSS PEYTON

"Oh my god. That was fun!"

I'd never worn a disguise before—how many people have?—but it was freakishly liberating. I was completely unselfconscious because I knew whatever bone-headed thing I might do could never be pinned on Joss Peyton, broke library assistant and sister to a soldier who'd gone missing.

Even if I weren't trying to evade some unknown enemy, this would still be cool as shit.

I made myself at home in the guys' suite after Thorn and I returned from our outing. What else was I supposed to do? They'd dragged me here, so I figured I'd make the best of it.

Arrow, clearly trying to intimidate me, stared me down while I pulled my wig off and started furiously scratching my head.

"My god, these things are itchy. How do people wear them all day?" She finger-combed her swingy black hair into place and wiped the pink stuff off her lips.

"You guys really shouldn't have gone out," Arrow grumbled.

Thorn threw his hands up in the air. "Look, it was fine. We just walked around the block and got a burger. She was completely unrecognizable. You have to admit it."

He shook his head. "You took a risk that was unnecessary."

Was he serious? Even though no one would have recognized me in a million years? Geez, these soldier guys really had some shit drilled into their heads.

I fought the urge to roll my eyes. "Okay. We won't do it again." I looked down at my hands like an ashamed little girl, and when Arrow saw I was mocking him, he stormed away.

Geez, that guy needed to take it down a notch.

My phone buzzed in my pocket, and I grabbed for it.

It wasn't Booker. I was stupid to hope it was.

Instead, it was my roommate, Sunday.

Shit. I'd sort of forgotten about her.

"Hi, Sunday!" I said in my cheeriest voice.

I pressed the *mute* button. "This is my roommate," I told the guys, then got back to the call.

"So, how are things, girlfriend?" I chirped.

She clicked her tongue and repeated herself. "Joss. Where the fuck are you, and what happened to our apartment?"

I'd been so wrapped up in my own drama that I'd forgotten to give her the heads up. What a shit I was. Our home was trashed because of something I was involved in, and my poor roommate had to bear the brunt.

"I know, Sunday, it's so horrible. Someone broke in"—the guys nodded their heads approvingly—"I can't imagine who might have done that. Is anything of yours missing?"

Her voice was breathy, probably from pacing the apartment and the shock of its condition.

I looked up from my Converse Chucks to see the three guys peering right down at me.

"Don't tell her anything," Arrow whispered.

I nodded.

Did they think I was a total dumbass?

"Yeah, I was so upset I couldn't even go to work. I'm um... at the mall right now. Pentagon City Mall."

She sighed. "Well, I think this place isn't safe. How bout I come pick you up and we go camp out at my parents'?"

I pressed *mute* again. "She wants me to go to her parents' with her. What do I say?"

Arrow just shook his head. "Think of something."

I took a deep breath. "Oh Sunday, what a great idea. You know, I think I'm gonna stay in town and clean the apartment up. Whoever it was, I'm sure it was a one-off.

We're super busy at work, and I don't want to bail on Candice."

Actually, I'd love to bail on Candice.

She hesitated, unconvinced I was making a wise decision. "Well, do you think the apartment is safe? I'm not sure how comfortable I am here."

I felt terrible. "Completely understandable, sweetie. Go to your parents. Let me deal with the mess."

The guys nodded.

I felt like shit for lying to my roommate. She'd been such a good friend to me, sex noise aside.

"Great job," Cruz said, patting me on the shoulder when I ended the call.

I laid my head back on the sofa. "God, it's just one lie after the other."

"True," he said, "but by being vague, you are keeping her safe. The less she knows, the better."

I couldn't shake my guilt, and that damn lump returned to my throat. "Do you think her life is in danger, too? Because of me?"

The guys looked at each other.

"She's probably fine."

Probably? What the fuck?

He must have seen the horror on my face. "Look, I am very... familiar with the kind of people we're dealing with here. They avoid collateral damage at all costs. It just leads to more trouble."

Is that what they called it? How heartless were these people?

"Well, I don't think of Sunday as collateral damage," I snapped.

I buried my face in my hands.

"Fuck, fuck, fuck. This whole thing is getting out of control."

Kneeling in front of me, Thorn took my hand. "They already searched your apartment and learned the bag was not there. They're not going back. They know you're one step ahead of them."

Ha. Me, one step ahead? That was a fucking joke.

I stood up, stretching. "Thanks for taking me out for a burger, Thorn. I'm tired. I'll see you guys later."

I passed through the open door adjoining our suites, and pulled it closed behind me.

Jesus, what was wrong with me? My hand was still tingling from Thorn's touch. And yet I couldn't get out of their room fast enough. I mean, these guys, soldiers of god-knows-what, were dangerous men. And while I'd enjoyed my time out with Thorn, he'd told me a story that scared the shit out of me.

Sporting my lovely disguise for our brief outing, we'd settled into a booth at The Old Ebbitt Grill. When he ordered a beer, I got one too. Organic, of course.

I had no idea there was such a thing as organic beer.

"So, what's your story, Thorn? Were you in the Army with my brother? Or did you meet him at The Company?"

Taking his glasses off, he smiled and tucked his messy hair behind his ears.

And holy shit, if I didn't almost drop my beer. I loved

guys with glasses, but this man was more beautiful than I'd realized under those thick specs and mop of hair.

He rolled his shoulders like he was getting ready for a long story. "First of all Joss, you know 'The Company' is not a real thing, right?" he asked, using air quotes.

I shrugged. "I really don't know much of anything about it at all. Booker always told me not to ask."

Yeah, and look where that had gotten him. My stomach twisted as I thought about what he might be going through. But I had to trust these guys were going to get him back. My awesome, annoying big brother.

"I… was recruited by the CIA right out of college. Actually, I didn't even finish my degree. I'd developed some software they found out about. They wanted it, and they wanted me. But when I realized the government's hypocrisy and non-commitment to making the world a better place, I bailed."

I had to laugh at that. People in Washington didn't talk about the CIA much, but when they did, it seemed like a place you were stuck for life.

"So," he continued, "I started working in private security around the same time your brother joined The Company, right out of the Army. They made us into… a different kind of soldier."

I sank my teeth into my bacon bleu cheeseburger. "Different? How?"

He gazed out across the restaurant. "We were warriors. Trained to kill and ask questions later."

Was he fucking kidding? My food suddenly tasted like cardboard.

"Um, what?"

"We were hired to do the work that governments and companies either couldn't—or didn't want to. Work that skirted the edges of the law. And ethics, some might say."

Holy shit. Maybe I was better off back at my own apartment, letting the guy with the bent wire-frame glasses do his worst to me.

Thorn continued. "My specialty was cyber, obviously, but you get trained for all sorts of situations. The government spent a lot of time and money training us, and when you leave, you're bombarded with offers from the private sector. Some of the things we ended up doing were downright criminal. It's very hard to go back to normal life."

That could not be what my brother did for work. He'd never get involved with anyone or anything shady.

On the other hand, would Thorn make up something so farfetched? And if so, why?

"We were paid well for it." He laughed ironically.

"And is this the sort of… thing that my brother did? Or *does?*" I asked, choking on the words.

Please say no.

Thorn pressed his lips together and looking down at his burger, ignoring my question. "So, I'm retired now. At least from The Company. I consult on all sorts of cyber shit, though. Keeps me busy."

And that was how I learned what Arrow, Cruz, and Thorn—and my brother—did for a living.

In the elevator on the way back, Thorn reached for my wig, tugging down the shaggy strands on either side of my head. "I think you're a little crooked here. Let me fix you."

Before he let go, he moved closer, brushing my cheek with his nose, then his lips, which found their way to my mouth. If I'd been paying more attention, I might have seen it coming. But I was so freaked about being in the company of three crazy soldier-warrior dudes, that I'd barely been watching where I was walking.

It was like he moved in slow-motion, touching me so lightly all I felt was his breath. And when he pressed his lips to mine, I nearly fell into his arms.

But as soon as the elevator doors opened, he freaked.

"Oh my god. I'm sorry, Joss. I shouldn't have done that." He zoomed down the hall toward our rooms, with me trotting to keep up.

My life was just getting weirder and weirder.

Why was he sorry he kissed me? Should I be insulted?

But he bolted into the suite before I could ask.

I'd had a nice time getting a burger and a beer, and I was especially grateful for the disguise, which, it turned out, was quite handy.

13

JOSS PEYTON

THE NEXT MORNING I WOKE UP—OR SHOULD I SAY, GOT
out of bed, because I'd really not slept all night—and
heard the guys in their suite speaking quietly.

So, equally quietly, I put my handy disguise back on,
and headed to work after leaving a note on my bed.

I knew they wouldn't be happy but Thorn had said I
was virtually unrecognizable with the wig, hat, and
glasses. And the library, where I'd take them off, would be
equally as safe because it was full of people coming and
going. No one would ever try anything there. It was so...
public.

Right?

Yeah, I knew the guys would shit, but I couldn't call in sick another day.

I texted Sunday to check in, although she was rarely up so early.

morning. heading to work

She surprised me with an immediate response. *omg. where were you last night?*

What? She knew I wasn't home? I thought she was staying at her parents'.

Think quick.

there's this cute guy at work I've kind of been flirting with

good for you girl. it's about time. you want a ride to work? I can come get you

Such a sweetheart.

on the bus. 2 blocks to go

ok. be careful. I called the police about the break in. they're coming over later

Oh shit.

But I had bigger things to worry about at that moment. In spite of my disguise, I couldn't help but look over my shoulder every couple minutes, as well as assess every new passenger getting on the bus.

Was this what my life was going to be like from now on? Maybe I should have just stayed at the hotel. The tension flooding through me made my neck and shoulders ache, and it wasn't even eight a.m. yet.

Just before I rounded the corner to the library, I pulled off my wig, hat, and glasses and stuffed them in my bag.

In spite of all that was going on, or maybe because of

it, it actually felt good to get back to the library. Things were predictable here. I had a routine.

"Look what the cat dragged in."

Did she really just say that?

"Nice to see you too, Candice."

I was so not in the mood.

As I was crafting my not-snarky response to her, we turned to watch the library's front door blow open. My heart jumped into my throat as a man with wire-rimmed glasses came in. Why had I thought the library was so safe? Why had I thought it was smart to leave the hotel?

Why had I thought it was okay to blow off everything the guys had told me for the past twenty-four hours?

But it turned out the man was just there to pick up the lunch box his kid had left behind the day before. He wasn't my would-be abductor. Not by a mile.

Candice sidled up to me. "He's nice looking, isn't he?"

"Who?"

She gestured with her chin. "Him. The dad who was just in here picking up whatever his bratty kid left behind."

I kept moving books onto my cart. "Um. Yeah, I guess."

She turned to fully face me. "Speaking of good-looking, how is that brother of yours?"

Really?

The mention of Booker sent a shiver up my spine. "He's fine, I guess."

She tilted her head, displeased with my non-answer.

"Now, Joss. No need to get snippy. I asked an innocent question."

I looked up at her and smiled. "You're right. Sorry, Candice. I'm just a little… under the weather from yesterday," I lied.

With one hand on her hip, she made it clear she wanted more information.

God, I wish I could just tell her to go fuck herself.

"I actually… haven't spoken to him in a few days. Not since he was last here. I think he's… busy."

I paused to see if that would satisfy her.

"What's he busy doing?"

Shoot me now.

"I'm not sure. But if you really want to know, I can find out for you." Maybe that would shut her up.

Her head snapped back on her neck. "Oh. Well. You don't have to do that. I was just curious." She turned on her heel and walked away.

Just curious, yeah right.

Her inquiries made my skin crawl, and I realized that maybe I needed to be watching her more carefully than I did the people coming in the front door.

∧

ARROW SULLIVAN

"Damn, Cruz, did you order every breakfast item on the menu?"

I watched as not one, but two carts of food were wheeled into the suite by a pair of matching bellmen.

He nodded, rolling up the sleeves of his plaid work shirt. "I am fucking starving. I didn't eat yesterday. Unlike *some* people." He shot a look in Thorn's direction.

"Hey, don't be hating on me because I spent time with our lovely new friend, Joss Peyton," he said, lifting the covers off the dishes one at a time to inhale the smells of bacon, eggs, and waffles.

"Yeah," Cruz continued, "I like how you pulled that off. Very sneaky."

Thorn shook his head. "Nothing sneaky about it my friend. But if you observe, you might learn from my technique."

They laughed and grabbed empty plates.

"God, this smells amazing," Cruz said. "I wonder if we should go wake Joss up."

That's why he'd ordered so much food. He wanted to impress Joss—make sure to get her exactly what she liked. I couldn't blame him, and I couldn't blame Thorn for whisking her away the day before, even though I thought he was taking an unnecessary risk in going out.

Truth be told, I wouldn't mind the opportunity to get to know her a little better myself. There was something about her that was just so kick-ass, like the way she punched the guy trying to kidnap her. Serious balls.

I figure she'd learned a thing or two from her brother.

Speaking of whom, I hadn't shared this with the guys, and especially not Joss, but I was getting worried about Booker. We'd made some progress assessing what he was up against, but things weren't moving nearly as fast as they should be.

And we all knew that the longer he was gone, the less likely it was that he'd be coming back.

But Joss knew none of this.

"It's nine a.m. I'm gonna go wake her," I said.

I rapped my knuckles on the door between our two rooms.

Jesus, was she still asleep?

I knocked again. No answer.

"Joss? Joss, are you up yet? We have breakfast over here."

"Maybe she's in the shower," Thorn said through his mouthful of waffles.

I pressed my ear against the door. "I don't hear the shower. I don't hear anything."

I really didn't want to barge right in, so I knocked one more time.

Nothing. With no other choice, I tried the door.

But it wouldn't open.

I groaned. I did not need any additional challenges that morning. "Shit. The door's locked. I thought we asked her to keep it unlocked in case we needed to get to her quickly."

Cruz crossed the room to me. "You don't think she's up to anything, do you? After yesterday's fiasco I'd think she'd learned her lesson."

Thorn came forward holding a room key card. "Relax, guys. Look what I have."

Jesus, he always managed to pull a solution out of his ass.

He headed for the hallway. "Let me go to the room's front door. Hold on a sec."

Our door slammed behind him.

Seconds later, I heard him opening the hallway door to Joss's room, and following that, he opened the door between our rooms.

There, Thorn stood on the other side. He did not look happy.

I pushed past him, and immediately understood his expression

She was gone. Joss was fucking gone.

"Jesus Christ," I yelled, furiously kicking a stray shoe in the middle of her floor. "What the fucking fuck? Is she crazy?"

While I continued my rant, Cruz held up a piece of paper he'd picked up from her bed. "She… went to work."

"Oh my god," I said, sinking onto the edge of her bed and burying my face in my hands.

It was one thing to save Booker, but to babysit his younger sister? I hadn't signed up for this.

"Fine. Fine," I said, popping to my feet. "She can run off, but if she gets grabbed again, it's her fucking problem. We can't be responsible for her stupid actions."

Cruz put up his hands. "Okay, Arrow. Take it down a notch. She's not doing this to purposely irritate you. She's scared shitless and is not making the best decisions. We've seen people in this situation before. We know how they behave."

I fell back on Joss's bed. I wanted to find Booker, get him out of whatever jam he'd gotten himself into, and get back home to New York. The stress of all this was bullshit. I'd retired with a nice, juicy bank account. I wasn't supposed to have to worry about another thing for the rest of my life, much less people who'd been kidnapped, or people who didn't care that they *might* be kidnapped.

Or even worse, killed.

Goddammit.

I pointed at Thorn. "You never should have given her that disguise. Now she has a false sense of security and thinks she can take off and do whatever she wants. We don't have the time to look after her while we're trying to find Booker."

My stomach churned at the thought that Joss's reckless behavior might pull us away from looking for her brother. I was indebted to that guy. We all were. And his life was certainly in graver danger than his sister's.

Unless she kept pulling her stupid bullshit, that was.

"I'll tell you what. As of today, let's divide and conquer. One of us will trail Joss to keep her out of trouble. The other two can focus on Booker," Cruz said.

Fine. Let him babysit the petulant brat.

He ran back to our room, rustled around, and returned with three straws.

We were going to draw straws? Really?

"Whoever picks the shortest is assigned to Joss."

For Christ's sake.

So, we drew. And don't you know, I got the shortest straw.

Was I pissed? Yes.

But was I also happy?

Yeah.

∧

15

ARROW SULLIVAN

I'D PRETENDED TO BE ANNOYED OUT OF MY HEAD WHEN I was assigned Joss detail, but the truth was, I pretty much ran down to the parking garage to my car.

What a fucking hypocrite I was.

What was it about her? She was a pain in the ass, no doubt, without much concern for how she was making our jobs tougher by not complying with our wishes. But, something about that also commanded respect. Well, to a point.

She wasn't playing victim. She didn't expect us to solve her problems. And while I wasn't on board with her approach, I had to hand it to her for sticking her neck out.

Booker would be proud.

If he ever found out, that was.

It took me only minutes to get to the Georgetown Library, and I left the SUV in a quasi-legal parking space.

I just didn't give a fuck at that point.

I had to make sure Joss was okay.

Running up the steps to the library, I took a breath before I entered. It wouldn't do to rush the place. This wasn't some kind of invasion.

And damn, the Georgetown Library was nice. I had to force myself to walk in like I was looking for something rather than gawking at the soaring bookshelves and oak paneled walls. There were patrons at nearly every table, some reading, some tapping on their laptops, and a couple dozing off. No one looked up when I entered.

Good sign. Nobody was on their guard.

But Joss was nowhere to be seen. Was I too late?

I ducked down an aisle to get the lay of the place, my heart thumping harder every minute I didn't set eyes on our girl.

Shit. Did I just say *our girl*?

Jesus, I was fucked.

A couple guys in skinny neck ties pushed carts of books around, presumably returning them to their shelves. A woman with overly bleached hair and a low-cut blouse stood behind the counter, helping a patron check out books, and a janitor lethargically pushed a huge, wheeled garbage can around, emptying the smaller ones at the end of every table.

I followed the shelves lining a wall until I reached the

very back of the library. There, I saw an open door, which revealed tables and chairs on a beautiful old brick patio surrounded by a lawn and giant oak trees.

No wonder Joss was so conscientious about coming to work. The place was freaking gorgeous.

And when I rounded the corner, there she was, reading to a group of little kids.

Perched in a child-sized chair, she was adorable as hell, of course, with her hipster hair, short dress, and Converse sneakers. About a dozen little faces looked up at her in wonder from their places on the floor. She'd read a page or two, then turn the book toward the group so the kids could see the pictures.

One of them raised a hand and asked a question I couldn't hear. But she answered the little boy with a kind smile, and got back to the story.

I'll be damned.

Now I knew why she worked as a library assistant when she had some fancy college degree—something I'd never bothered to earn. She liked the work. It was rewarding.

I'd been a problem child, and sent to a military school for a good part of my education. As much as my parents thought it would prepare me for college, the only area where I really excelled was in skipping class and marksmanship. In fact, I was so good at shooting that The Company recruited me right after graduation, and put me through their soldier training program. Fortunately for me, they turned a blind eye to my truancy issues.

I learned that the training I faced was multiples harder than what you got in the Army. Which was fine because we got paid multiples more for our efforts.

But the shadow work we did got to me after a few years. I had all the money I needed in offshore accounts, so I retired.

Private security, a euphemism for many things, was a young man's job and didn't leave anyone unscathed. I still had regular nightmares, and walked with a slight limp from being shot in the hip. My days were now spent partying in New York City with my buds and fucking pretty women.

Not the most meaningful of lives, but it helped me forget some of the shit soldier life had thrown my way.

Joss closed the book she'd been reading to the kids, who were starting to be claimed by their parents. She patted the little ones on the head as they left, then started cleaning up.

I'd have been lying if I didn't say I was impressed. I was also sorry I'd bitched about her. She deserved all the protection we could offer.

"Joss," I whispered, hoping it was loud enough for her to hear without drawing attention.

She looked around, and I finally caught her eye. Her mouth dropped open, then she smiled.

"Well, look who it is," she said, fake surprise crossing her face like she didn't know at least one of us would come after her. "Are ya mad?" she asked flirtatiously.

Jesus. Had she just batted her eyes at me?

God, I didn't need this woman flirting with me. I had a fucking job to do.

"Arrow," she said in a quiet voice after looking around, "now you see why I can't blow off my job. People are counting on me."

Jesus Christ. I wanted to lecture her and tell her that if she turned up dead, all those people who were counting on her would be shit out of luck. That her brother, if he survived, would never be the same if he lost her. And that Thorn, Cruz, and I would never be able to forgive ourselves.

But instead, I just leaned toward her and kissed her.

I think I was just as surprised as she was, but I didn't care. Her lips were soft under mine, and when I pressed them harder, she leaned into me. But I stopped when a movement caught my eye.

"Who is that?" I whispered, pointing at the woman behind the desk, now running around like a busy bee.

"Oh. Shit. That's my boss. Gotta go," she said, turning away.

But I grabbed her arm before she could. "Tell her you don't feel well. I've got to get you out of here. I'll wait at a table."

Exasperated, she sighed. "Why?" she hissed.

I gave her a stern look. "Just do it. Trust me."

I walked to the other side of one of the bookshelves and pretended to be looking for something so I could hear Joss speak to her boss.

"Oh hi, Candice. Great group of little kids, huh?"

"Mmmm hmmm."

Guess she wasn't much for praise.

"Hey, I'm still feeling under the weather from whatever I had yesterday. I need to go home."

Her boss was silent, then sniffed. "Well, if that's what you feel you have to do."

"Thanks for understanding, Candice. I hope there isn't something going around."

The woman wrinkled her nose at the suggestion that she might catch something. "Me too. Hey, who was that handsome man you were just speaking to?"

Oh shit. Had she seen us kiss?

"The tall guy? I don't know. He was just looking for a book on... naval history."

That actually sounded like something I might like.

"Where did he go?" the boss asked. "I wouldn't mind getting to know him better."

So, Joss's boss was a horny man-eater. Too bad she wasn't a nicer person—she might actually get some action.

Although, not from me.

I pulled a book off the shelf to pretend to read and made my way to a table where I could oversee everything, avoiding the gaze of the horny librarian.

I had work to do and my number one priority was to get Joss someplace secure.

Well, I had other priorities that involved her, too.

Those would have to wait, but hopefully not for very long.

16

JOSS PEYTON

"Joss, could you shelve these books before you go? Should only take five minutes."

I could be throwing up blood and the woman would not give a shit.

For dramatic effect, I let my shoulders slump. "Sure, I can do that. No problem," I said in a weak voice.

If I were going to fake sick, I'd better act sick.

I pushed my cart across the library, and when I was sure Candice wasn't looking, made my way over to where Arrow was pretending to read.

"How's your book?"

He snapped it closed. "No idea. Too busy watching the

goings-on. This is a busy place." He gazed around again, and I realized I knew that look.

He was scanning. He was always scanning. All the guys were. I'd seen my brother do it too. I'd always thought he just wasn't interested in what I had to say when he looked into the distance in the middle of one of our conversations.

Watching everything around him was an ingrained behavior.

I pointed at the cart. "My boss wants me to shelve these books. Shouldn't take long."

Nodding, he opened his book back up. "Have at it. I'll keep an eye on things."

I headed over to non-fiction and, passing various patrons browsing the stacks, started with the biographies that needed shelving. For whatever reason, they'd been extra popular lately.

The first one I picked up was a new book about Lady Diana Spencer. After making sure Candice wasn't hawk-eyeing me, I flipped through it while scooting out of the way of a smiling man passing me in the narrow space between towering shelves. I could use something good to read in my swanky hotel room, so put the book back on the cart to check out before I left. I grabbed the next book, and as I did, a slip of paper floated off the cart and to the floor.

I looked at it before I bent to pick it up. People used all sorts of random stuff as bookmarks, and were forever leaving them in the books they returned. I'd found tissues, dry cleaning receipts, a break-up note, a business card for a strip club, money, and even a mini-pad. Unused, of course.

Fortunately, this bookmark, a little folded piece of paper, looked relatively harmless. I bent to retrieve it, and because I was in the mood to be nosy, opened it up.

Big mistake.

I started shaking so badly, I had to lean on the cart to stay upright.

I looked around frantically for Arrow, but in the far corner of the library all I could see was towering shelf after shelf of books. Even the man who had just squeezed by was nowhere to be seen. So, leaning on the cart, I propelled myself back to the front desk.

"Doesn't look like you're done," Candice quipped after eyeing my cart.

I didn't have to fake sick now. "I... I'm leaving," I stumbled.

I looked up to see the man who'd just been in the stacks with me bolting out the door. After a quick glance over his shoulder at me, he was gone.

Had he left me that note?

Candice jumped off her stool and took a couple steps back to put some distance between us. Her eyes widened like I'd turned into some sort of monster. "Oh my *god*. You look horrible. Leave, before you make anyone else sick."

So compassionate.

I grabbed my jeans jacket and purse, and as I passed Candice, pretended to stifle a weak cough.

"Excuse me," I rasped, just to be a shit.

I raced toward Arrow and, catching his eye, nodded toward the door. As soon as I was outside, I opened the slip of paper again and put my hand over my mouth, this time, to stifle my cries.

Arrow joined me seconds later. "What the hell—?"

I thrust the paper at him and watched his eyes narrow.

"Fuckers," he growled.

I looked one more time, and I vowed not to again because I would otherwise lose my shit. The slip of paper had a picture of my brother tied to a post, bruised and bloodied, and said:

Your brother for the bag.

I gagged and ran down the library steps to the sidewalk where, if I really got sick, I could aim for grass or a tree.

I'd known Booker was in trouble. That didn't come as a surprise. But seeing it right there, in living color, was a different sort of reckoning.

These people, whoever they were, could have the goddamn bag. The consequences of that, whatever they might be, were of no concern to me. I just wanted my brother. And to be left alone to go back to my apartment with Sunday, and to gripe about my boss in peace.

Was that too much to ask?

Arrow's showing up at the library had been... expected, but not exactly appreciated. But now I was grateful. I wasn't sure I could even navigate the bus home if I had to at that moment.

Where was home, anyway? The freaking Mayflower Hotel?

"Oh my god, Arrow. What should I do?" I sobbed quietly. "Look at Booker. Just look at him."

My brother. When we were kids, he'd hold things I wanted just out of my reach to aggravate me. That's how I got so good at slugging.

Now, I'd do anything to have him tease me again.

Arrow grabbed my hand and we headed for his car, not quite running but certainly not walking, either. He loaded me in the passenger side and we took off, screeching down Wisconsin Ave.

"Arrow, how… how are we supposed to get the satchel to these people if we don't even know where they are?" I wailed, hiding my face in my hands.

He reached across the console and stroked my hair. "They'll provide instructions. They're just trying to freak you out. Where did you find the note?"

"Some man dropped it off on my cart. I didn't actually see him do it, but I'm pretty sure he was the one. I was shelving books, and he came down my aisle and had to squeeze by. I didn't even look at him, I was flipping through a freaking book about Lady Diana. But before I left, I saw a man hurrying out the door who looked back at me and took off. I think it had been him."

"What did he look like?"

Of course, he was going to ask that. The problem was,

after a while, all library patrons looked alike. "I don't know. Normal. Tall, thin, dressed conservatively. He looked like every other guy on the streets of DC."

Arrow nodded. "Probably just a courier."

"Why are people so hell-bent on getting that stupid bag? It only has gym clothes in it."

"Sometimes there is more than meets the eye."

Λ

17

JOSS PEYTON

"Just… try to relax a little, if you can."

I settled onto a sofa back at the hotel, and I scrolled through my phone to call Sunday. I had to make sure she was okay.

"Hey, hold up," Arrow said. "Who are you calling?"

I held the phone up, now ringing. "My roommate, Sunday."

"Hang up. Hang up now," he growled.

Sunday answered on the first ring. "Hey, Joss!" It was so good to hear her voice.

But before I could say anything, Arrow was across the room. He grabbed the phone out of my hand and hung up the call.

"What the fuck?" I snapped.

He raised his hand. "Hold on."

He could fucking hold on. I was not.

I got to my feet to reclaim my phone.

But he held it out of my reach. "She'll call right back. Tell her the call was dropped. Don't tell her anything else. At all. Say you're at your mother's. That you had to use your vacation time."

And just like Arrow had said, my phone started ringing, the screen lighting up with *Sunday Jones*.

He returned it to me.

Jerk.

"Sunday! Sorry 'bout that. Damn dropped calls," I said cheerfully.

"Oh, no worries, sweetie. Hey, you haven't been by the apartment. It's still trashed."

Shit. I'd promised to clean it up.

"I know, I'm so sorry. I needed a little break from the city so I'm at my mom's using my excess vacation time."

She was silent for a moment.

"Sunday? Are you there?"

She laughed. "Yeah, yeah. Sorry, I'm trying to parallel park."

Arrow leaned toward me from his chair, where he was watching my every move. "Finish the call," he whispered. "Tell her you have to go."

I rolled my eyes, and he reached for the phone.

But I swiveled before he could get it. "Sunday, gotta go. I'll call later."

And I hung up.

"*What* is with you? I can't even talk to my friend?"

Arrow took a deep breath. "At this point, we don't know who we can trust—"

"Oh c'mon, Arrow, she's my freaking roommate. Next thing I know you'll tell me not to call my mother."

He nodded. "You're catching on now."

"Huh?"

He came over to the sofa and sat down next to me. "We don't know who the other side might have gotten to. It's better to be safe than sorry."

Shaking my head, I looked down at my hands. "I just don't understand this world. And I don't understand why my brother is part of it."

Arrow shocked me by reaching for my fingers, but his hand felt so good, I gripped it back. It was soothing and strong. Like everything might be okay.

Which I knew was wishful thinking.

And then I remembered his earlier kiss at the library.

What the hell was wrong with me? My brother's life was on the line, and I was thinking about the hot guy next to me. Whose friend I'd kissed the day before, by the way.

But how could I not? His dark eyes drilled into mine like he could see right through me, and now that he was so close, and getting closer, I could enjoy his simple, clean scent—

So with no one else around, I went for it. I needed something to take my mind off the shitty day, and if that involved a gorgeous man, then so be it.

I put my hands on either side of his face and brought my lips to his, brushing them back and forth at first, then leaning into him when he pressed my mouth harder.

I wanted to melt into this man and forget about the shit swirling around me. When he wove his fingers into my hair, I was pretty sure I was on my way.

He leaned me back onto the sofa and hovered above me, supporting his weight on one arm. Our legs tangled, and it didn't take me long to realize he had an erection.

"You're very pretty, you know."

"Thank you," I whispered.

With his gaze on mine, he unbuttoned my blouse to just below my bra, and ran his fingers along its lace so lightly I gasped, shivering in goosebumps.

"You're so hot," he murmured.

I pulled away from him for a second. "I have to tell you Arrow, that I kissed Thorn just the other day."

He dropped his head with a small laugh. "I know. It's cool. We're not possessive guys."

He knew?

But before I could think about it further, he pushed the lace down on my bra and encircled my nipple with his tongue, tasting and teasing me until I found myself arching into him for more.

"Mmmm…" I moaned.

He reached for my other breast and lightly pinched my nipple, twisting it just enough to reach the border where pleasure turned into pain, and they blended together so there was no beginning or end to either one.

"I need you to fuck me, Arrow," I murmured, surprising myself.

He smiled down at me. "Yeah?"

Reaching into his back pocket, he retrieved a condom, then pulled my jeans below my ass. Before I could even think about it, he flipped me over on my stomach, parted my legs as much as possible while they were still bound by my jeans, and drove his tongue into me.

He groaned. "Tastes so good."

Behind me, I heard his jeans open and a condom roll along his length. He put his knees on either side of my hips, and with a strong hand, lifted my ass into the air.

He leaned over me as his cock bounced at my entrance and whispered. "Are you ready for me, baby?"

Jesus, was I ready. I didn't even care that the other guys could wander in at any second. I wanted to be filled with this man.

"Yeah. Please fuck me, Arrow," I whispered.

He entered me a couple inches and paused, thank god, because he was much bigger than anything I was used to. I bit my lip to keep from crying out, and dug my nails into the sofa below me.

"You okay?" he whispered.

I waited a moment longer, until the initial burn faded, and nodded. "Yes. It's okay now."

He eased the rest of the way inside me and held himself there until my rasping breath got normal again, and then slowly pulled out and pushed back in.

I'd never felt so filled, and now that the initial pain had

faded away, I wanted it hard and fast. Bound by my blue jeans and Arrow's knees on either side of my hips, I could barely move. In fact, I was kind of trapped, but I pushed my ass back enough to let Arrow know I was ready for more.

He began to piston my pussy harder and faster, and the tingle that had started in my core flamed through me, followed by an explosive orgasm that left me pounding the sofa.

Moments later, Arrow pushed inside me one last time. "Fuck, baby, I'm coming," he groaned loudly, pulsing deep inside me.

After we caught our breath, Arrow got me to my feet and helped me to my room. He undressed me and put the fluffy white down comforter over me and kissed my forehead.

"Promise me you won't lock the door between our rooms."

I nodded and turned onto my side, sleep being the second-best thing for running away from one's problems.

18

CRUZ DUFRESNE

"Holy shit, Arrow, someone really gave Joss this picture of her brother? That's fucked up."

Thorn stared at the piece of paper I'd passed him, shaking his head.

"I agree. It's pretty damn aggressive. They are clearly getting desperate for whatever it is they're after," Arrow said.

I went over to the suite's safe, opened it, and returned with the cross-body satchel that had been at the center of Booker's disappearance.

I set it on the table in front of us. "Why would they want a bag that just has gym clothes in it?"

Arrow turned the bag over and examined it from

several angles. "Whatever it is they want, it's not fucking gym clothes."

I watched him examine the bag, as we all had countless times already. "After all that went down today, Arrow, I'm thinking Joss is not safe here in DC. What do you think about having her come to the ranch in Montana? It's doubtful they'd think to look for her there."

Thorn nodded. "That might be a good idea. You take her back to Montana while Arrow and I work on finding Booker."

I couldn't deny it, my pulse kicked up at the thought of bringing Joss home with me. She was a cool, kick-ass woman, and I'd love to show her what ranch life was all about. I was also dying to kiss her if she were open to it.

I was pretty much an evangelist for the simpler life. Unfortunately, so far, no amount of convincing had swayed Arrow from New York, or Thorn from San Francisco, even temporarily. But I held out hope that they'd at least let themselves enjoy the ranch once or twice a year.

I'd love to show it to Joss if the timing were right.

"On the other hand, guys," I added reluctantly, "since whoever is trying to get to her is being so persistent, maybe it's best to keep her here in order to lead us to Booker."

"Why is my door open?"

We whipped around to see Joss standing in the doorway that joined our rooms, wrapped in an oversized hotel bathrobe, her hair sexily tousled.

And pissed as hell.

"This door needs to stay open, Joss. We can't risk having you sneak out again," Thorn said. "Sorry."

He wasn't sorry. None of us were.

She glared at him. "What? That's bullshit."

I stood to try to diffuse the situation. "Now, Joss, if you'd just listen—"

But when her face turned bright pink, I knew an explosion was imminent.

She entered our suite, arms swinging. "It's one thing to be here in this hotel, and I appreciate all you're doing for my brother and me, even if it sometimes doesn't seem like it. But I need a certain amount of privacy. This open door idea… goes too far."

I raised my hands. "You'll have all the privacy you need, Joss—"

Not good enough.

Her voice got louder. "Why can't we just give that goddamn bag to the people after it and get my brother? It seems like a simple exchange to me, and I don't know what's taking so damn long, or what's so complicated about it. In fact, if I'd hired you guys, I'd fire your asses right now."

Damn. If she wanted us out of her life so badly, I was inclined to say *see ya*. But I couldn't turn my back on Booker. None of us could.

Nor could we turn our backs on her, as tempting as it may be.

I ushered Joss back to her room before one of us said

something we regretted. "Can we talk?" I asked quietly, taking a seat on the edge of her bed.

She stared at me, hands on hips. "What?" she hissed.

Jesus, she was mad.

I patted the spot next to me. "Come here, please."

She rolled her eyes and stormed over.

"I want to tell you a story about your brother, Joss."

She plopped onto the bed like a sulky child. Who knew Booker had such a pain in the ass sister? A *cute*, pain in the ass sister?

Difficulties aside, she had a lot to learn about her brother.

"When we were with The Company, your brother and I were in a foreign country—I can't tell you which—on a stakeout, watching some… bad guys. They finally came flying out of the house we were watching, guns blazing, just as a little girl chasing her ball ran down the sidewalk."

Remembering that day made my stomach clench, as it always did. There was collateral damage, and then there was *collateral damage*. The kind that will haunt your dreams for the rest of your life. Private ops soldiers like us know it comes with the territory, but we always hope we won't have to face it.

Her eyes widened. "Oh my god. What happened?"

"Well, we're never supposed to break our cover. It could risk the entire mission. But your brother did, just this one time. He leapt out of position and grabbed this little girl just as she skipped into the line of fire. He narrowly missed getting shot and killed, but he saved this kid. It was… like a miracle."

Booker, with his typical modesty, had insisted it wasn't a big deal, but I couldn't call it anything else. I'd seen it with my own eyes.

Her mouth hung open.

As I thought it would.

"That's not the only heroic thing your brother has done, but this one, in my mind, is probably number one. The chances of his coming through that alive were very slim. Afterward, he said he knew your dad would be proud, if he were alive."

"My dad? What does my dad have to do with it?" she asked, confusion crossing her face.

"Well, you know when your dad—"

But I stopped.

She didn't know. She didn't know about her dad's work for The Company.

Seemed it was time for her to find out.

"Joss, what do you know about your father's death?"

She swallowed. "Um, well, he died in a car accident when he was traveling for business. In Malta."

"Not exactly. Joss, your father worked for The Company, which your brother joined after his death. Booker wanted to carry on his work."

Her pretty face was covered in confusion, and she shook her head.

I got it. She didn't believe me. Shocking news takes time to sink in.

"No, Cruz. My dad worked as an imports broker. He helped foreign companies navigate getting their products into the country."

That was one of the best covers I'd ever heard. But it wasn't true.

I just looked at Joss, who I imagined was reconciling all the lies she must have been told over her lifetime. But they'd all been to protect her. She had to know that.

After a minute, she looked up from the hands she'd folded neatly in her lap. "So… you're saying my dad didn't die in a car accident?"

I thought carefully how to answer this, considering how much Booker would want her to know. But she was involved now, and needed to know the stakes.

"It probably wasn't an accident, Joss."

She looked back at her hands until her shoulders began to shake. Tears fell onto her bathrobe as she quietly cried.

"Do you think he was afraid? Do you think he suffered?" she asked, looking up at me with a face distorted by tears.

I pulled her to me. "I am sure he died bravely. He was trained for it. And… I'm sure he was sorry he'd never see Booker or you again."

When she put her hand to her mouth to stifle another sob, I pulled her to me and she collapsed in my arms.

"Oh my god, I never knew. My poor father," she sobbed.

Fuck. This was the worst part of our business. And it

was why I'd gotten the fuck out of it. When you're a soldier, it's not just hard on you. It's hard on everyone around you.

Thorn came in with some peppermint tea. "Here you go, sweetie," he said. "This may make you feel a little better."

She let go of me and took a long inhale of the steaming tea. "Thank you."

She turned to me. "See, I told you I'd have no privacy. The guys over there heard every bit of our conversation."

I had to laugh. That was the least of our damn worries. Arrow had been to a warehouse where he thought he'd find Booker just this morning and had hit another dead end. I was beginning to wonder if we'd been out of the business too long for our old contacts to have anything really useful for us.

In fact, at least half our contacts were unreachable. They were most likely living off the grid in some faraway country—or were dead.

Joss sighed, apparently all cried out. "This tea is good. But now my head is killing me. I might lie down for a bit."

I helped her under the covers and drew the curtains shut. Before I left, I sat next to where she lay.

"Need anything else?"

Fuck, she looked so small and vulnerable, the information she'd just received having knocked all the bad-assery right out of her.

Temporarily, of course.

"I'm okay. I guess. Hey, when my brother came by the

library to drop off the bag, I saw him ride off on a motorcycle."

"Yeah? So?"

She frowned. "Well, I've been thinking about this. Maybe you can shed some light. You see, he wasn't into motorcycles. He never liked them. And he's never owned one."

Another new bit of information for our girl to absorb.

"He might not have liked them, but we're all trained to ride them. They make for very fast get-aways. We all had them when we were with the company. He probably just never told you."

She shook her head.

I reached for her hand. "You're really something, Joss Peyton, you know that?" I said with a laugh. "Just as gutsy as your father and brother."

She gave me a small smile. "I'll take that as a compliment."

"You definitely should."

She reached up and pushed my hair behind my ears, something easy to do since I'd grown it out after my days with The Company. Her touch was soft but confident, and before she could take her hand back, I grabbed it and kissed her fingers, one by one.

I worked my way into her palm, then up her arm, now bare since she'd removed her bathrobe. When I reached her shoulder, I lingered there for a moment, then brushed my lips over her neck and up her chin.

And when I finally reached her lips, she was ready for me, kissing me back with all the fervor I'd hoped for.

Now, I wished the door was closed. In fact, I got up, walked across the room, smiled at the guys on the other side, and quietly closed the door.

Fuck the rules.

I lay her back on the bed and kissed her with more urgency, probably because I'd been waiting to do so.

"You're beautiful, Joss," I breathed, sprinkling kisses over her temples, and working my way down her shoulders.

"Thank you, Cruz," she whispered, her fingers scraping through my hair.

Damn, she felt good, and it was my plan to let her know how much I appreciated her. I moved my way down her body, past the little tank top she slept in, which barely contained her breasts, to the lacy panties covering her sex. I eased aside the crotch to access her pretty pussy, and dipped my tongue into the slit between her lips.

"Oh god, Cruz, that feels so nice," she mumbled.

"Good baby. I want you to feel good."

I slipped a finger inside her and started a 'come here' motion that I knew, coupled with the pressure of my tongue, now on her clit, would bring her to an earth-shattering orgasm.

It didn't take long.

She began to tremble, and her breath came hard and fast. Her head bucked against the bed, and she thrust her hips against my face.

"Oh… oh, yes, I'm coming, I'm coming…" she muttered, shuddering under me.

A minute later I whipped my erection out of my pants and moved to straddle her. Pushing her tank top out of the way, I jerked myself until I came all over her pretty tits.

My release was a badly-needed one, and when I was done, I collapsed next to her on the bed, pulling her into my arms.

∧

19

JOSS PEYTON

I AWOKE IN A FOG, MY ROOM DARK, AND I HAD NO IDEA what time it was. One thing I did know, however, was that I was alone.

I'd nodded off with Cruz, but he was no longer there.

I slowly pushed myself up in bed, and with the door open between our rooms, I could see the guys' suite was quiet.

I found my robe on the floor and pulled it on while I made my way to the window. I pulled the blackout curtains open a crack, and was nearly blinded by the sunshine.

Okay. It was clearly daytime. I hadn't been asleep that long.

I wandered over to the suite, and found remnants of the guys' lunch. There was one extra plate with a dome over it, I assumed for me, so I lifted the lid and found a nice, thick BLT. I was actually starving and sank my teeth into it. Before I knew it, I had devoured half the sandwich.

Good of them to think of me.

They really were a nice bunch of guys, and not just because I'd messed around with all three of them. Well, I'd only kissed Thorn, but I'd done the deed with Arrow, and now Cruz.

Were they going to think I was some kind of hussy slut? I hoped not, but if they did, tough shit. I didn't owe anything to anyone, and as long as I was stuck with these guys, I might as well have some fun.

I'd lived like a nun for far too long. Time to take a page out of Sunday's playbook.

Speaking of Sunday, I ran back to my room to call her while the guys were out. I was sick of having them eavesdrop on my calls.

"Joss! Where the hell have you been?" she demanded the moment she answered.

I pulled the curtains in my room all the way open and lay back on my bed. "Oh my god. Life has been crazy, girl. I'm not supposed to tell you, but I'm holed up with three of my brother's friends. Apparently, he's in some kind of danger, and they feel compelled to protect me, too."

While I was flapping my gums, Arrow's words pecked at the edges of my conscience.

Don't tell her anything. It will keep her safer.

Fuck. I needed to shut up, right now. I couldn't put her in danger and possibly subject her to the bullshit I'd been going through, or what my brother was going through.

"Oh my god. What are you saying, Joss? What do you mean *danger*? How are they *protecting* you and where? And does this have to do with our apartment break-in?"

Shit, shit, shit, why did I open that can of worms?

"Oh, Sunday, I'm sorry. I didn't mean to make it sound that bad. And… it *may* be related to the apartment break-in," I lied.

What an idiot I was.

"Joss, *where* are you? I'm coming to get you."

I sighed. "I'm sorry, Sunday, but I can't tell you any more than that. I won't be going back to work for a while either."

This part of the whole thing sort of broke my heart. As annoying as my boss was, I loved the library. It had become my sanctuary. I missed its orderliness and quiet beauty.

"That is bullshit, Joss. You'll come with me to my parents'. You'll be safe there."

"Ugh. I wish I could, Sunday. I'm dying to see you. But I can assure you, I am safe with these guys. And on the bright side, they are hot."

Sunday clicked her tongue. "I'm happy for you," she said sarcastically.

Geez. I thought she'd be more interested than that.

"But tell me, what *are* they like?" she asked, her tone turning saucy.

Ha. I got her. Any mention of three good-looking men got Her Royal Horniness all worked up.

I looked around to make sure I still had the place to myself. "Well, one of them is from New York, kind of preppy with short hair and a beard. Tall and buff. Another has a ranch out West, so he's all rugged and tan from being outdoors. He has this really cool dirty blond hair with streaks from the sun."

"Oh my god," she breathed. "A guy with a ranch?"

I laughed, the ugliness of my situation slipping away, if only for a moment. "Yeah, can you believe it? I never met anyone with a ranch. Then, there's the last guy, who lives in San Francisco. He's kind of a computer nerd and wears these really big, black eyeglasses and has his hair pulled into a ponytail, like a mad professor. But he also has these dimples and full lips, and when he smiles, I could just faint."

It felt good to dish with Sunday, even if I wasn't supposed to. A girl can't live by bread alone. So to speak.

Maybe I could sneak out and at least have a drink with her—

Just then, I heard the guys at their door.

"Sunday, I gotta go. I'll call you later."

"But wait, Joss—"

I jumped off my bed and grabbed some jeans and a T-shirt and ran into my bathroom, the only place where I had real privacy.

"Hey, guys," I hollered before I shut myself into the bathroom.

"Hey, Joss," they called.

A few minutes later, I came out and was heading over to get the second half of my BLT when I noticed something had been slipped under my door. I scooped up an envelope with the hotel's logo on it, figuring it was the bill or something, and joined the guys in the suite.

"Whatcha got there?" Thorn asked, pushing up his nerd glasses. *Hot* nerd glasses.

I turned the envelope over to open it while I munched on my sandwich with the other hand. "I don't know. Let's see."

I clumsily pulled a piece of paper, also on hotel stationery, out. I shook it open and promptly dropped it on the ground.

"Oh my god. Oh my god. It's another note."

Arrow was across the room in two steps. "Holy shit," he said, reading it.

"How... how..."

I couldn't even form a sentence.

Arrow knelt in front of me. "Go fill up a duffel bag. We've got to get you out of here."

But I barely heard him. My head was spinning.

How did they find me here? And were they just outside my door? On the other side of the wall? Waiting for me?

"What the hell is it?" Cruz said.

Arrow read:

*The bag for your brother. Time is running out. Don't be stupid
if you want him to live.*

"Can't… can't we just give them the bag, guys? Please?
Then this will all be over, right?" I stumbled.

"Joss, the minute they get the satchel, they'll kill both
you and your brother, and possibly us as well. These are
not nice people we're dealing with," Thorn said.

Well, fuck all. Things were even worse than I knew.

"C'mon, everyone. Pack a few things. We are leaving in
five minutes," Arrow said.

Thorn and Cruz hustled to their rooms, probably
accustomed to this sort of life. I, however, was not.

So, Arrow gently grabbed me by the upper arm and
propelled me to my room.

"Where's your bag, Joss?"

Paralyzed with fear, I looked toward the closet.

Arrow pulled out my duffel and put it on the bed.
"Joss, snap out of it. Put some clothes and your toiletries
in the bag."

When I just stood there, looking at him, he got in my
face.

"*Now!*" he yelled.

That woke me up.

I ran to the bathroom and scooped everything I had
scattered on my vanity into the plastic laundry bag
hanging in my closet. Then, I tore open one dresser
drawer after another and stuffed their contents into my

bag. I was just reaching for the last drawer when Thorn came in and grabbed my bag.

"Hey! I'm not done."

He tipped his head at me. "Yes, you are. Let's go."

I peeked into the suite, where the other guys were waiting by the door, bags thrown over their shoulders.

How the hell did they do that?

I glanced around the room one last time, grabbed my sketch book, and ran after them.

In the elevator on the way down, the guys formed a triangle around me like they were Secret Service and I was the president or something. I felt sort of important, but also sort of like a poseur. I was a nobody and they knew it.

When we reached the lobby, the cheerful concierge ran out from behind her desk. "Miss Peyton! Oh Miss Peyton!" she called.

I turned around and the guys moved closer to me.

"Hi. What can I do for you?" I asked.

I'd been here for only a few days and she somehow learned my name?

She jumped up and down a little.

"Did you see your brother?" she asked, grinning.

I looked at the guys, who didn't take their gazes off her. "Um… no. Did you?"

"Oh darn." Her face fell. "Guess you guys missed each other. He came in and was so cute. He explained it was your birthday and that he wanted to surprise you with flowers.

But you know, we're not allowed to give out room numbers, but when he showed me his ID and some photos of you guys when you were kids, well of course, I believed him."

She looked at the four of us, thrilled by her efforts.

But when no one smiled back, hers slowly faded. "Um, is everything okay?" she asked.

I nodded, and without a word, Thorn put his arm around my shoulder and we kept moving toward the parking garage.

"Oh, Miss Peyton, happy birthday, by the way," the concierge sang after us.

No one said a word until we got in Arrow's SUV.

"Guess that was where the note came from," Cruz said.

What in the fucking fuck was going on?

Arrow screeched out of the parking garage and sped toward Highway 50.

"Wh… where are we going?" I said in a shaking voice.

"To the Eastern Shore of Maryland," Arrow said. "There's a house there where we will be safe."

Great. Just great.

In spite of all that was going on, the guys looked business as usual. Had they done shit like this before? Was this considered normal in their world?

All the warmth of my conversation with Sunday, and my sexy time with Cruz seemed like they were just a dream. They'd never happened, and I was stuck in this hell of uncertainty, being hunted by an unknown entity, threatening both my brother and me. All over a stupid cross-body satchel.

"Where's the bag?" I mumbled.

"We have it," Thorn said, reaching across the seat and taking my hand. "Why don't you try and relax a little? We'll be there in two hours."

I looked out the window and opened my sketch pad to see if I could draw while the car was moving. "Where are we going?" I mumbled.

We entered the highway, and I realized Arrow was passing all other traffic. A quick look at the speedometer showed he was going northward of ninety miles an hour.

Jesus, was he crazy?

"We're going to Kent Island to a safe house compound. You'll like it there, it's on the water. Very comfortable."

I'd never been to Kent Island, only driven through it on the way to the beach.

"Whose house is it?"

Cruz looked over his shoulder from the passenger seat and smiled at me.

God, he was cute. I exploded in goosebumps reliving his kiss. And other things.

"It belongs to one of our... associates. That's all you need to know," he said.

Well, all right then. We were going to a safe house, presumably to be safe. But for all I knew, we were moving further away from wherever Booker was, and further away from freeing him from his captors.

"What about Booker?" I asked in a quiet voice.

I had to force myself to say the words. I was so afraid

the guys would say there was nothing they could do, or it was too late, or that they'd made no progress.

I braced myself for the worst.

"We haven't told you, Joss, because it was iffy for a while, but we think we know who has him and where he is," Cruz said.

"Yeah, some of our contacts are still useful after all," Arrow added.

I nearly jumped through the roof. "Are you kidding? Are you fucking kidding? Why didn't you tell me? You jerks!"

I slugged Thorn in the arm since he was closest.

My brother would be proud.

∧

20

THORN JENSEN

"THORN, DON'T YOU THINK IT'S MESSED UP THAT I'M HERE in this beautiful place while my brother is holed up god knows where?"

Joss's shoulders slumped as we followed a sandy little path toward the waters of the Chesapeake Bay.

I threw a casual arm around her. I'd been hoping for a reason to.

And she wasn't kidding about beautiful. As 'safe houses' went, the one where we'd just arrived was pretty fucking amazing.

In between dozing, I'd watched the scenery of DC, and then Maryland, whiz by for two hours until we hit the iconic Chesapeake Bay Bridge. While I hadn't been there in a few years, driving over that sky-high monstrosity never ceased to amaze. Even Cruz sank down in his seat up front, pretending to read something on his phone.

Arrow was the only one not even slightly bothered. I counted that as a win since he was the one driving.

Taking the first exit off the bridge, we traveled down a vaguely familiar country road until we hit a big, official-looking gate with cameras covering every possible angle. I glanced over at Joss, sitting next to me in the back seat. Her eyes were wide as she took in the significance of the compound—pretty out of place on the quiet little island.

The gates swung open, and we followed a long, dirt road through a tunnel of trees until we reached a stone house with more cameras, all aimed at the drive and the front door.

Yeah, my people liked their cameras.

"It's amazing," Joss said, opening her car door before we'd even fully stopped.

"Wait till you see the inside," Arrow said, grabbing her bag.

He wasn't kidding. The compound on Kent Island was breathtaking. I could see Joss sharing the same reaction. The entryway led to a sprawling living room with multiple seating areas, the largest one clustered around a fireplace. What was most breathtaking, though, was the far wall of glass, providing a view of a beautiful patio and the Bay beyond it.

I still had no idea whose house this was. I didn't want to know, either. It didn't matter.

And I wasn't going to ask. Although Joss would be full of questions, no doubt.

"When we free my brother, can we bring him here? He'd really like it."

If memory served, Booker had been here plenty of times. But there was no reason to go into that now. "Don't see why not. He'll probably need a nice little rest."

Cruz threw me a look. The place was a safe house, not a vacation resort.

At the mention of her brother, sadness washed over Joss's face. It wasn't hard to see the toll worrying about him was taking. Hopefully, the peace that the safe house offered, which she so desperately needed, would melt away some of the tension that had been knotting her up since the day she realized he'd gone missing.

Booker's foresight in alerting his sister, and us, amazed me. He was freaking lucky as hell he'd realized things were closing in to the point where he had to take the drastic measure of involving her, especially when she didn't even know what he did for a living. I knew him well enough to know he wouldn't take that lightly. In fact, wherever he was captive right now, he probably had a heavy heart about dragging her into his world.

It was a damn good thing she did contact us right off the bat rather than look for him herself. She probably wouldn't have succeeded in doing much more than getting the both of them killed.

And even if she acted like our protecting her was some sort of prison sentence, in time, she'd realize the restrictions placed on her were a small price to pay in exchange for her life.

All too often in this business, when shit hit the fan, the soldier targeted never sees it coming. Those sorts of losses were always devastating to The Company. Booker was lucky this time. He might not be the next.

But I was sharing none of that with Joss. I had no desire to send her deeper into despair. In fact, I considered it my personal mission to cheer her up.

And maybe have a little alone time with her.

"Let's go for a walk," I said to Joss, gesturing outside.

Her face brightened as she looked at the rippling bay water, and she followed me to the house's beachfront.

We sat on a rickety dock that predated the house, no doubt built years ago when the property was inhabited by the watermen who made their living fishing and crabbing. Dangling our feet over the shallow water, the peace was disturbed only by the occasional screeching seagull.

Joss looked over at me. "You know, Thorn, I wanted to tell you… that I've… been with Arrow and Cruz."

That was what had been on her mind?

Trying not to laugh, I took her hand and turned my gaze back to the horizon. "I know."

She had so much to learn

"Oh. Really?" She giggled nervously. "Well, I… um… hope you don't think that's skanky. Or anything like that."

Was she kidding? Did she think we were fucking Neanderthals?

Now, I turned to face her. She needed to see how

serious I was. "Why would that be skanky? Arrow and Cruz are awesome guys. And you're an awesome woman."

I thought she might drop it right then, but she kept going. Which was good. I wanted her to talk about it.

"So... have you guys done this kind of thing before? You know, gotten together with the same woman?"

I nodded. "Yeah, in fact we have. It's hot as shit."

She was trying to play it cool, but it wasn't hard to see she had a thousand thoughts racing through her head.

We were different from the guys she usually met, there was no doubt about that. In fact, we were different from *most* of the men out there. We'd all made different choices than the average guy. And none of us regretted it.

At least not too much.

"But I have to admit, Joss," I said sheepishly, "I haven't been with anyone in a while."

Fuck it. Why should I be embarrassed about that?

She tilted her head. "Really? Any particular reason?"

Taking off my glasses, I dropped them into my shirt pocket and rubbed the bridge of my nose. I didn't share my story with many people, but I figured Joss deserved to know it. "I went through a nasty divorce a couple years ago. I've dated a little, but haven't really had my heart in it."

Her eyebrows rose with surprise. "Gosh, I'm sorry to hear that."

"Yeah. I was sorry, too. Didn't see it coming, like a lot of men. I wasn't paying attention to the signs. And my wife's pleas for changes. See, when I was with The

Company, I wasn't around much, and some of the shit I saw stayed with me even after I got home. I just wasn't really there for her."

The understanding on her face gripped me. Even if she hadn't experienced it herself, I'd had a feeling she could understand deep remorse.

"I guess there was no mending things?" she asked.

At the time, I would have done anything to make that happen. But as situations like that usually go, the opportunity to repair things had passed by the time I realized anything was broken.

"No. I'd basically ruined things. It's why I left The Company. I was paid well, but money isn't everything. Lost my marriage."

She ran her hand over my back, which was amazing in the warm afternoon sun.

"In the divorce, I gave her everything. I figured she deserved it for putting up with me and my lousy attempt at being a husband."

I swallowed away a little lump in my throat. I didn't cry. At least not if I could help it.

"That's why I'm doing the cyber consulting now. I don't have the nest egg Arrow and Cruz do. But that's okay. I'll catch up."

Yeah, I'm sure Joss thought I was nothing more than some computer geek who sat in his Victorian house in San Francisco writing code all day, occasionally getting food delivered so I didn't have to leave the house.

It's funny, the assumptions you make about people.

I took a deep breath. "I haven't felt attracted to anyone. Until you."

Her face turned a bright pink. "Thank you," she murmured.

She looked like she wanted to dive into the Bay to put the fire out.

But I continued anyway. "I know I kissed you the other day, but I'd *really* like to kiss you again."

"Then what are you waiting for?"

∧

I EXTENDED my hand to help Joss to her feet. About halfway up the path we'd just descended, we ducked into a small clearing covered in soft pine needles.

She did a full three-sixty to take it in. "How did you know this was here?"

I led her to the spot's one bench, still bathed in the late afternoon sun. "I came down here once to read. It's a nice, quiet place when you want some time to yourself."

"So peaceful," she breathed.

I followed her gaze straight up at the canopy of trees towering over us, throwing off a fresh, piney scent.

I turned toward her and with my hands on either side of her face, ran them lightly over her cheeks, down the back of her neck, and up through her hair until I held fist-fuls of it.

Her eyes fluttered closed as I hoped they would. She softened under my touch, the warmth of the sun, and the light lapping of the Bay as the tide came in. I wanted to take her away from her worries and to a place where everything was fine in the world, where the only thing to do was enjoy the nature surrounding us. And because that wasn't possible, I was determined that we both enjoy the moment as long as we could.

My fingers slowly tightened on her hair until her head was forced back into the perfect position for a kiss.

I was already miles away, and I was taking her with me.

21

JOSS PEYTON

UNLIKE THE FIRST KISS I'D HAD FROM THORN, WHEN HE WAS just exploring, the force of this one took my breath away. I gasped when he pulled back to look at me, still not releasing my hair, but rather pulling my head back even further so he could run his lips over my neck.

I'd never experienced someone who was soft and aggressive at the same time. I didn't even know it was possible. And as I caught my breath, I found I was both scared and turned on as hell. I wanted him to touch me all over like that, leaving his trail of fire on every bit of my skin until I exploded.

With shaking hands, I unbuttoned his shirt and then mine, just in time for him to push mine down my arms and reach behind my back to open my bra. With those things out of the way, he stood me up and pulled my jeans down to my ankles, helping me step out of them.

I was now completely naked, outdoors, and with a man whose tender power both intimidated and exhilarated me. There was something so freaking dominating about being undressed and regarded as if I were nothing more than an object, especially when I couldn't do it back, in return.

Thorn, wearing just enough of a smile that his dimples made my stomach clench, traveled my bare skin with his intense gaze. How could someone be so freaking cute and also devastatingly manly at the same time? The collision of his disparate sides made me ache, starting at my core, and radiating to my every last inch.

He laid me back on the bed of pine needles and hovered above me, running his lips over my breasts, down my stomach, and to my sex, where he kissed all around, avoiding my core, and driving me freaking crazy. It was all I could do not to spread my legs and shove his head between them.

But when I thought about it, would that be so bad?

Turned out, I didn't have to wait long.

With the last bit of the afternoon sun hitting us, he pushed my knees up to my chest, baring my most private parts.

And I loved it.

I wanted him to see me, to know me, and to enjoy me, as if those were my gifts to him. He was special in many ways, and I wanted to cement our connection beyond his protector role.

It was so odd. I barely knew him, and yet I felt like I'd do anything to please him.

And with his arms rigidly holding me open, he studied me from my ass to my clit and back, as if he were memorizing the sight. Or, trying to torment me. Which he was doing very well.

Finally, he ran his tongue through my slit, mixing my cream with his saliva and sending shivers through my body. When he saw my hands fly to my tits, which I pushed together and kneaded hard, he let out a low groan.

"Fucking hot, baby," he murmured.

He cautiously slipped one finger inside me and then another, scissoring them as if to explore my walls, and, I suspected, stretch me. I didn't know what his plans for me were, but I knew what I was hoping for, and I prayed I wouldn't have to wait long.

"Pussy tastes so good," he said, pulling back and letting my legs go as he slipped a finger in his mouth.

He reached into his back pocket, retrieving a condom, and opened his jeans to pull out the thickest cock I'd ever seen.

While I was staring at the monster I was afraid might actually hurt, he lay on his back and pulled me on top. But before he sheathed himself, he had more instructions for me.

"Okay, baby, face away. Like reverse cowgirl."

I flipped, facing the other direction, the anticipation

heightened because I couldn't see behind me. I heard the rolling of the condom and then felt his hands on my hips holding me close to his cock.

"You ready for me to fuck you?" he breathed.

Holy shit. Was I ever.

"Yeah," I mumbled.

"Okay. Lean forward. Put your hands on my thighs. I want to watch my dick fuck you."

Jesus. I placed my hands just above his knees, my position pushing my ass up and opening me as wide as I could be.

With one hand on my hip, he slowly impaled me, inch by inch, until he was fully seated. When he was all the way inside, he held himself there for a moment.

I'd be lying if I didn't say it was uncomfortable, the stretching of my inner walls. But after a few deep breaths, the sensation turned into a pleasant throbbing, and I gripped him on my way to orgasm.

I'd never been one to come fast, but I had a feeling that was about to change.

A feathering tingle built in my lower belly and gradually rose as I began to slide on and off Thorn's dick. With my hands on his legs for purchase, I had the perfect leverage to fuck him exactly as I needed to satisfy myself, which was reacting like a hungry, greedy little animal.

"Goddamn, baby," Thorn growled, "I love watching your pussy take me. You're so open, babe, it's fucking hot."

He gathered my wetness on a finger and spread it on my asshole.

Damn. He was really going there.

And I was fine with it.

While I milked his cock, one of his fingers plunged into my ass in a brutal thrust. I screeched, probably loudly enough to be heard up at the house. The pain in my behind was a sharp contrast to the pleasure in my pussy, and was just enough to send me over the edge.

Bouncing on Thorn like my pussy was starving, my orgasm blasted me. I gasped for air, the effort stripping my throat dry.

"Oh fuck, baby," he shouted behind me.

His finger withdrew from my ass and with his hands on my hips, he held me on his cock while it pulsed deep inside me. I could feel his shuddering, nearly matched by my own, as my pussy contracted for another orgasm.

Suddenly, there was a sound in the bushes. I jumped off Thorn, but with my wobbly legs, fell right over.

Thorn shot up, an old instinct, I was sure, and we watched Arrow poke his head into our clearing

"Anybody hungry?" he asked with a big-ass smile.

Λ

22

JOSS PEYTON

DAMN THESE MEN. THEY WERE SO DIFFERENT FROM THE usual DC weenies I met, who only talked about their jobs and where they went to school. My soldiers—if I could call them that, it sounded so freaking hot—were worlds away from that shit. And if they did half the crazy stuff Cruz told me my brother had, well they had me hook, line, and sinker.

"Oh my god, what smells so amazing?" I asked, lifting the lid on a pot simmering on the stove.

These guys could cook? Was there nothing they weren't champs at? It wasn't fair. Like the day the universe made them, it was on a perfection streak, and that afterward, there was none left for the rest of us.

We sat down to a dinner of braised short ribs, cheddar grits, and greens on the side. I didn't think I'd ever eaten anything so delicious. But I also suspected my appetite was heightened by my incredible encounter with Thorn.

And the amusement of having Arrow catch us.

I kept stealing looks at him across the table, wondering what his reaction to our session was going to be, and when he finally caught me, he winked and smiled.

And of course, showed off those blasted dimples.

My face felt on fire while I blushed up a storm.

Arrow saw us flirting. "So. You guys had fun down by the bay today, huh?" he asked with a friendly smirk.

Thorn raised his eyebrows at his friend. "Jealous much?"

Oh my god. I was embarrassed but also ready to explode in the company of these three beautiful men.

"What about you, Joss? You have a good time?" Cruz asked.

All eyes turned my way, so I stopped the fork halfway to my mouth, trying to think of a way to crawl away in shame without being noticed. It took me a moment to realize they were teasing the shit out of me, and when I finally laughed, they joined me.

So, I decided to be a smart ass right back. "It was okay," I said, rolling my eyes.

Thorn coughed hard, muttering *"bullshit,"* which got everyone rolling.

Cruz leaned back in his chair and stretched, his arms

spread wide. "I don't know about all of you, but I'm still a little hungry."

Arrow was skeptical. "What the hell dude? You had two helpings of everything."

Thorn laughed. "Arrow, I don't think he means hungry for more *food*."

Oh my.

"You know, I could really use some dessert, myself," I said as coyly as possible, resisting the urge to jump one or maybe even all of them.

Cruz walked around the table and took my hand while Arrow took the other. As they led me to the living room, I looked back over my shoulder at Thorn, who gave me a shit-eating grin, and began to clear the dinner dishes from the table.

In front of the large window, a full moon shone down on the water, its light breaking into pieces as it was disbursed by the rippling bay. Arrow lowered the living room lights and the moon seemed to get brighter, illuminating the three of us as the guys sandwiched me. Cruz took my front side, and Arrow the back, and I was instantly transported to some sort of heaven when their four hands began to roam my body.

Trembling with want, I closed my eyes and swayed with their movements, not worried about losing my balance, so tightly pressed I was between the two. Arrow's hard cock drilled against my butt cheeks, igniting the bit of soreness Thorn had left me with. He picked my hair up off my neck and ran kisses along my collar line, leaving me convulsing with the occasional shiver.

Cruz, in front of me, had already opened my blouse and had each of my nipples between a thumb and forefinger. He pulled on them gently while his mouth explored mine, so unselfconsciously confident it nearly made me faint.

How did I get so lucky, I was wondering when an uninvited thought flashed through my mind, reminding me that in a few days I might never see the guys again. It was probably for the best, because once my brother was safe, all the time I'd spent with them would have to be on the down-low.

Booker would not be happy that his friends were fucking me. Or that I was fucking them.

But, for the time being, I was pretty happy about it.

"Are you ready to suck some cock, darlin'?" Cruz whispered into my ear.

I nodded, incapable of much more than that.

"Yo, Thorn. Can you bring us a dining chair?" he called.

I heard some furniture shuffle. "Coming right up," Thorn replied.

I opened my eyes to see Arrow had pulled out his cock and was stroking himself slowly. With my free hand, he led me to the dining chair Thorn had brought. He had me kneel on it, facing the back of the chair.

For a moment I wondered what they were up to, but it became clear pretty fast.

I was now at the perfect height to take his cock into my mouth. I opened wide, like a hungry little bird and waited for him to fill me. His hands settled on either side of my head, and his big dick landed on my lips like a tease.

In the meantime, behind me, Cruz pulled my jeans to just below my ass and bent over as I was sucking Arrow, my backside basically in the air.

Because my jeans weren't pulled down far, my legs were essentially bound together. Cruz helped himself to my ass cheeks, parting them with a low whistle, and plunged a finger into my pussy.

I pushed back against him, I was so hungry for more.

"Fuck, man, she's ready," he murmured.

A third pair of hands smoothed over my back, which must have been Thorn's. I was so glad he'd joined the party.

I would have told him… but my mouth was full.

"Look at that little pink rosebud," Cruz said.

"Mmmm. It's nice. I was in there earlier today."

They were talking about me like I wasn't even there. Which was hot as fuck.

"Dude, you gave it to her in the ass?" Cruz asked disbelievingly.

Thorn laughed. "Yeah, but just with my finger. I definitely think she's ready for more, though."

Oh my god.

With Arrow in front of me, holding my face in a vise-like grip while he fucked my mouth, and Cruz behind me pressing my backside, I was completely pinned. With the exception of a little slack, I couldn't move forward or back.

Not that I wanted to.

"Do me a favor, Thorn," Cruz said, "and open her cheeks a bit for me."

Thorn's hands flew to my ass. "Happy to assist," he said cheerfully.

If I didn't have a mouthful of cock, I would have laughed out loud.

But what came next wasn't much of a laughing matter. Cruz or Thorn—I wasn't sure which—spat on the crack of my butt and dragged the saliva down and over my asshole. Tickled by the familiar feeling of that afternoon, I felt myself tighten to ward off any invasion. But when a tongue circled my ass, I groaned and relaxation began to wash over me.

After a minute, the tongue was replaced by the head of a cock. As memory served, he was big, and I had no idea how the hell he thought he'd get that in my backside.

But he somehow did.

"Okay, Thorn, you got her cheeks?" he asked.

"Yeah," Thorn rasped. "You're gonna take her with no lube?"

Jesus, I was in trouble. I wouldn't be able to sit later.

"Oh yeah, she'll be fine. The condom will take care of it. See, she's relaxing already," he said as his cockhead slowly stretched me open.

I wasn't sure a condom was going to make it easier for him to penetrate my ass, but I was in no position to argue.

"Push back out, baby. That will help," he said, his hands encircling my waist.

I did as he asked, and while it hurt, his head popped inside me.

Even with a full mouth, I had to grunt in response to the pressure at my back door. I had no fucking idea how he'd be able to go any further, but it turned out, once the head was in, the rest just followed.

Next thing I knew, my bottom was filled with a big, fat cock. Cruz pumped me slowly at first with tiny little pulses, until he could slide in and out with little resistance.

At the same time, Arrow bellowed and pulled out of my mouth. I'd wanted to swallow his cum, but it seemed it was his preference to come against my cheek.

He spurted endlessly, rubbing his last few drops over my lips, which I eagerly licked. He moved behind me, I imagined to watch my ass get fucked by Cruz's monster dick.

"Holy fuck, that's beautiful," he said, still catching his breath.

Another pair of hands landed on my ass cheeks, parting them enough so everyone could see my bottom being invaded.

And just when I thought I couldn't take another pump, a shiver shot up my spine, and I exploded in an unexpected orgasm.

I gripped the chairback that I was draped over, my

breasts bouncing and my head bucking, screaming things I don't even remember.

One last thrust by Cruz, and he rammed his cock deep inside me one last time, bellowing and exploding in my backside.

I was completely delirious, my senses screaming so loudly I couldn't see, hear, or think a goddamn thing. I wasn't sure who, but one of the guys led me to my room, where I had a private bath. He filled it with hot, sudsy water, and helped me into it.

Kissing me on the head, he lowered the lights. "I'll be back in fifteen minutes. Holler if you need anything."

I leaned my head on the back of the tub, sank as low into the water as I could, and replayed every second of the last hour.

23

ARROW SULLIVAN

Goddamn Joss.

We'd pretty much fucked the stuffing out of her. I had to half carry her to the tub, and when I returned to help her dry off, she'd fallen asleep in the still-steaming water. I lifted her out, balanced her on the edge, where she sat with her head hanging down on her chest, and briskly dried her.

"You okay, sweetie?" I asked.

"Mmmm," she said, nodding happily.

"C'mon. I'm putting you to bed."

When she was snugly tucked in under her fluffy down comforter, I bent to kiss her goodnight and turned to leave.

But before I could, she caught my wrist. "Stay," she said, simply.

Hmmm. I hadn't considered that. "Are you sure?"

She nodded. "Get in."

Well shit. I didn't need to be asked twice. I stripped down to my boxers and crawled in, wrapping her exhausted body in my arms.

Joss mumbled something I didn't catch.

"What's that, baby?"

She took her face out of the pillow so I could hear. "Why are you always so grouchy?"

Oh. That.

Not the first time I'd been asked that question. Well, maybe not that exact one, but I knew what she was getting at.

I pulled her closer, her skin still deliciously warm from the bath. "I don't know that I'm grouchy, Joss. Just maybe not as… accessible as the other guys."

She snorted and burrowed back into her pillow.

Christ, was I that bad?

"Okay. Maybe I'm not as warm as Mister Rancher or Mister San Francisco. That's what happens when you live in New York City. I'm just kind of… to the point. No messing around. No fluff."

"Well, why do you live there? Why don't you live someplace… easier?"

Ah, the question non-New Yorkers loved to ask. And the real answer was one that only made sense to us crazies who lived there.

"It's one of the best places in the world to disappear. I don't mean entirely, like off the grid, but if you're wanting to forget who you are and start over, it's a good place to be. People don't ask a lot of questions."

I didn't mention the plethora of gorgeous women in New York who kept my bed warm at night who also made it a delightful place to live. But Joss was at least as beautiful as the women at home, and she wasn't out to land a wealthy husband like many of the ones I met.

This intrigued me. She was suffering through a somewhat crappy job, for which she was grossly overqualified, and yet was still determined to show up at work every day out of some inexplicable loyalty. Her brother had dragged her into an unfortunately dangerous mess, and she wasn't intimidated by it.

And she handled the three of us pervs like the champ that she was.

"Arrow?"

"Yes, beautiful?"

She flipped over to face me, and I pushed her dark hair out of her face. "How long do you think we'll be here?"

I took a deep breath. "I don't know. I'm sorry."

She shrugged and turned back over. "Okay. Well, I signed up for another drawing Masterclass. I've already taken a few."

That's what I liked about this girl. She was determined to make the best of a shitty situation.

Moments later, she was breathing evenly, so I slipped back out of the bed and joined the guys in the living room. I wouldn't have minded turning in for the night with our lovely girl in my arms, but we had work to do.

Thorn and Cruz were sprawled on the living room's matching sofas with beers in their hands, so I grabbed one for myself from the fridge and joined them.

Thorn looked around. "This place is so fucking awesome. I could almost be tempted to give up San Francisco if I could hang out here full time."

"You wouldn't last five minutes here, dude. Looking at the bay is nice, but that's *all* there is to do," I said.

Thorn laughed. "Spoken like a real New Yorker."

I took a swig of beer. Christ, it was nice to kick back, even if only for a short while. If all went according to plan, we were going to hit the ground running in the next couple days. Word had it from our contacts that they'd discovered who was holding Booker and were close to identifying his whereabouts.

"This has been a good mission, guys. It's kind of nice to get back in the game. When I hung my hat up a few years back, I figured I'd never see any of your ugly faces again," I said.

Cruz laughed and held up his beer. "Cheers, assholes. Life wouldn't be the same without you. I didn't think I'd ever be doing this again. I was so done with The Company. But I will say it was sure as hell better than the Army. Jesus, my first year I was shot twice and couldn't even afford to replace my old pickup truck."

"Enter the private sector," Thorn said. "Always ready

to capitalize on the time and money the government spent training us."

I nodded. "Yeah, they got their money's worth out of us. But in the end we did okay."

"Well, except for me. I'm starting over, but my current gigs do not put my life in danger. That's always a nice bonus," Thorn said.

"Speaking of bonuses, who knew Booker's little sis would turn out to be such a honey?" I said, lowering my voice.

I couldn't let her hear us talking about her in case she woke up. None of us wanted to be labeled a big mouth scumbag.

Even if we were blathering on about her.

But how could we not?

"Oh my god, that was so fucking hot. Not that I liked looking at your dick, Cruz, but seeing her take it—"

Cruz held his hands up. "No need to recap, Thorn. I don't think we'll ever forget that fun little session."

Fuck, I hoped there'd be another one soon. My dick was rock hard even thinking about it. The way she'd gazed up at me while sucking me off…

"Arrow. *Arrow*," Thorn said, snapping his fingers.

"Oh, sorry. Lost in thought."

He smiled knowingly.

"Yeah, and I bet I know just what you were thinking about. Shit, if I were local to DC, I'd be all over dating Joss. What about you guys?" Thorn asked.

Cruz and I both nodded. "Of course, I'm interested. We all are. We're not fucking idiots."

"So, let's all date her," Thorn said. "People do that shit in San Francisco all the time."

Cruz tapped his chin. "The question is, would she be interested in such a… unique arrangement?"

"How would it work with us living all over the country?" I asked.

"And what would Booker say?" Thorn added.

I threw my arms up. "Only one way to find out. We'll ask her."

I went to my room and retrieved Booker's satchel, which had started this whole thing, and the matching one we'd found at the store that morning to use as a decoy.

I dropped them both on the coffee table in the middle of the room and gestured. "Check it out, Thorn. When Cruz and I went to the store earlier—"

"You know, when you were fucking Joss," Cruz interrupted.

Thorn raised a finger in the air. "Oh yes. Now I remember." He shook his head, amused.

"Okay kids, let's stay on topic," I chided. "As you can see, we have a decoy satchel that's exactly like the one Booker gave to Joss for safe keeping."

Thorn picked them both up. "Holy shit. The only way I can tell them apart is that the original one has the gym clothes in it."

He played with the bags, zipping and unzipping to check them out.

And then he stopped.

"You know guys, something about this one is different," he said, holding up the original.

"How so?" Cruz asked.

He dropped the new one on the table, and ran his fingers along the padded shoulder strap. "Look. Compare this."

The original bag had a logo tag sewn on the strap. The new satchel's tag was on the inside of the bag.

He looked in the old bag to see if it had an interior tag, like the new one did.

It had been removed.

And it appeared to have been re-sewn onto the thick shoulder strap.

Cruz reached into his pocket and passed Thorn a folding knife. "Here. Pry up the stitches."

Thorn opened the knife's smallest blade and picked at the stitches holding the tag to the strap. When he'd torn through a couple, he was able to grip the tag and pull it away.

With the tag removed, a hole remained. He dug his fingers inside it, moved them around, and he held up a small piece of plastic.

"Holy shit. This was here all this time and we had no idea," he said, shaking his head.

Cruz squinted. "Jesus Christ. Is that a thumb drive?"

"Yeah." Thorn jumped from his seat and returned with his laptop. After a few clicks on his keyboard, he slipped it into a port on the side.

I was short on patience that day. "What is it? C'mon."

Thorn frowned. "Well, it's password protected. It might take me a while to get into it. But this was what Booker was hiding in the bag. He sewed it into the strap and covered the hole with a tag."

Jesus. How many times had we scoured that bag and not realized we were looking right at what Booker was hiding?

"What do you think is on it?" Thorn asked.

"Whatever it is, people are willing to kill for it," I said.

"It's got to contain names, either of people on our side or people on the other side. That's the only thing that would be so valuable that Booker would put his life on the line," Cruz said.

Holy shit. It was probably a list of Booker's informants. There'd been a leak somewhere along the line and the enemy—whoever that happened to be—had discovered that not only someone on their side was feeding information to the outside, but also that Booker was the recipient of said information.

Talk about a big fucking security breach.

"That's how Booker's handler ended up dead. They probably went to him and when they realized he wouldn't help, figured the only way to get what they needed was to kidnap Book."

I put my head in my hands. "What a mess. But guys, this is a good find."

Thorn looked up from his laptop. "I say we don't share this latest find with Joss. I think the less she knows at this point, the better. She's already gone through so much."

"I agree. The less she knows, the less valuable she is to whoever's looking for her," I said, yawning and stretching.

If I didn't get to bed soon, I'd be spending the night sleeping in a chair in the living room, that's how close I was to falling asleep.

"Guys, I'm exhausted."

Cruz smiled wickedly. "Guess Joss wore you out, huh? Better work on that stamina, dude."

I flipped him the bird. "My stamina is just fine. In fact, I think I'm going to go test it right now, just me and my hand."

"Oooh, sounds romantic. Arrow has a date with his hairy palm," Thorn teased.

I dropped my head back and laughed. "I'll bet a hundred dollars both you assholes will be doing the same thing when you turn in tonight."

They looked at each other and nodded.

I knew it.

That Joss. Every time I was with her, instead of satisfying my itch, I ended up just wanting more.

And if all went according to plan, there would be more. Much, much more.

∧

24

JOSS PEYTON

"Wow. What smells so good?"

Cruz came out of his room in his PJ bottoms and some seriously sexy bed head. I was about to comment, but kept my mouth shut. I didn't want him to fix it before I admired it for a while.

I waved with my spatula. "I am making us a nice, big country breakfast. Since we're out in the country and all."

Arrow and Thorn joined us, most likely lured out by the bacon I was just beginning to take off the stove. "Have a seat everyone and I'll start serving. Coffee's on the table with the eggs, and I'm about to bring over the pancakes."

"Holy cow," Arrow said. "What a nice thing to wake up to."

I glanced at him in time to catch his sexy wink. I couldn't lie, I crawled into bed with him in the middle of the night and 'accidentally' woke him up.

Whoops.

"Where'd all this stuff come from?" Cruz asked, marveling over the feast.

I set down the last platter of bacon and joined the guys. Just looking around the table made my heart flutter.

"I woke up early and couldn't get back to sleep, so I ran out to the store."

I braced myself for the scolding.

The languid expression on Arrow's face morphed into something just short of anger. "You *what?*"

I waved him away. "Look. It was a quick trip to the grocery store and back. I wore Thorn's Army jacket and my disguise. You said yourself that no one knew we were here. So what's the harm?"

The guys just looked at each other.

Shit.

Arrow took a deep breath like he was composing himself, but I knew that was just a front for his coming explosion. "Joss, do you want to die young or something?"

I laughed and stuffed a piece of bacon in my mouth. "Oh my god! How did you know?"

Even after our recent sexy time, this man still needed to chill out a little.

Just then, there was a loud crash as Arrow brought his fist down on the breakfast table so hard it rattled all our dishes and sent the coffee in each of our cups splashing onto the table.

"Jesus, Arrow," I snapped, dabbing at the mess. "Nobody knows we're here. And I wanted to do something nice for you guys."

"You might *think* no one knows we're here, but you don't know that for sure." Scowling, he turned back to his eggs.

I wasn't going to argue. I didn't see how anyone would find us here, but I was willing to drop it. Unless the guys had told someone we were here.

Would they have done that when they'd insisted no one could be trusted?

So ridiculous. I mean, I'd told Sunday where we were, and I was about to tell the guys that, when I decided to keep my big mouth shut. I didn't need to give them anything else to get pissed about.

Although I did feel strongly that someone needed to know where I was, which was why I'd told Sunday. She'd agreed I'd be safer here, and told me to relax and have a good time if I could.

When all this was over, maybe she and I could look for a new apartment. Next time we spoke, I'd bring it up. Start fresh in a new place that had not been broken into.

You'd think Arrow might be a bit more chill since I'd given him a nice little surprise in the middle of the night. But I guess not.

After his outburst, the table was silent except for the

sounds of silverware on plates and food being passed around.

Whatever.

No one was going to ruin my good mood.

I'd gotten up in the middle of the night to use the bathroom and passed by Arrow's door, left slightly open. Of course, I poked my head in to take a look and found the full moon casting light on his gorgeous naked body, sprawled across the top of his sheets.

I had to stifle a giggle when I saw a handful of crumpled tissues next to him. Seemed my friend Arrow still had a little fuel left in his tank from earlier.

Which was when I got an idea. I crept over to him, but stopped. What if I startled him and he attacked me or something? Weren't these guys trained for this sort of thing? You know, kill and ask questions later?

I'd been watching too much TV.

But because I preferred my neck unbroken, I approached the bed, staying just out of his arms' reach.

That way I could at least make a run for it if he came after me.

"Arrow," I whispered.

Nothing.

"*Arrow*," I whispered louder.

He grunted and rolled over, his magnificent ass now facing me.

God, I was dying to run my hand over that mound of muscle. But because I valued my life, I kept my hands to myself.

For the moment, anyway.

"Arrow," I said, this time not whispering.

He flipped over in bed and sat up, looking around the dark room. "Who's there?" he growled.

"It's me," I said quietly.

He dropped his head back and took a deep breath. "Joss. What are you doing in here?"

Now that the danger of a broken neck had mostly passed, I got closer. "I don't know. I was just walking down the hall and saw your door open."

"Really? Was there also a big sign that said *come on in even though Arrow's sleeping?*" he snapped.

I tried to stifle a giggle at his crankiness, but it didn't work. Pretty soon I was shaking with the laughter I was trying to contain and had to put my hand over my mouth.

"Jesus Christ," he grumbled. He peeled the covers back as an invitation.

So, I joined him.

"Hey, Arrow. What are those tissues from?" I teased. "They're practically glowing in the moonlight."

Yikes. I was really pushing it.

And while it was too dark to see the expression on his face, I was pretty sure he rolled his eyes.

"What the hell do you think they're from, Joss? Would you like to inspect them?" He gathered them off the bed and chucked them onto the floor.

I giggled again. God, this guy was going to think I was a big pain in the ass. If he didn't already.

"No thank you, I do not really want to inspect your

tissues. But I can think of something else I'd like to inspect."

As he lay facing me, I smoothed my hand down his chest, over his stomach, and found his cock, raging hard like I hoped it would be. I wrapped my fingers around it and stroked it to the root then back up to the tip.

He groaned, his earlier irritation magically forgotten, and reached for my tits. "Fuck, baby, that feels nice."

"Yeah?" I whispered. "You like how I'm taking care of your hard cock?"

He let out a long exhale. "You have no fucking idea," he murmured.

I increased the speed with which I was pistoning him while he plunged his cock deeper into my grip. He moaned, his body convulsing. Warm semen pulsed into my hand and when the stream stopped, I reached for the tissues that were conveniently placed on the nightstand. Before I'd even finished cleaning us both, Arrow's breathing had settled into a slow rhythm, and I immediately followed him to sleep.

So, while the glow of his hand job the night before might have faded because I'd been a bad girl and run out to the store that morning for breakfast, at least I was still smiling from it.

Thorn put his hands up and looked around the table as if to assess whether a peaceful conversation could be had. I guess he figured the storm had mostly passed because he moved on to the next subject.

"Joss, we guys were talking about you last night, and wanted to propose something."

I laughed. "What's that? You want to lock me in my room so I can't skip out again?"

That didn't earn me any laughs. Whatever.

"Nothing like that," he said patiently. "We all… that is, the three of us… like you. We'd all like to date you."

I almost dropped the forkful of pancakes I was about to stuff in my mouth. I looked from one guy to the next, and they all looked right back at me.

God, they were beautiful, and all in such different ways with Thorn's hippy-nerd vibe, Arrow's clean-cut style, and Cruz's rugged outdoorsiness. I'd date any of them, given the chance, but there were a few factors working against us, not least of which was that I didn't live anywhere near any of them, they were my brother's buddies, and there was no fucking way a woman could date a posse of friends.

Was there?

"Yeah, very funny," I said with a roll of my eyes.

Hopefully, they couldn't see past my effort to play it cool, when I was really ready to melt into a huge puddle of need right there in front of them.

"It's not a joke, Joss," Cruz said. "After this mission, Arrow and Thorn were considering moving to the ranch. You could come, too."

I looked at Arrow. "Mister New York, leaving the Big Apple? Yeah, like that would ever happen."

Arrow's face had softened from his earlier rage. "I'll be keeping my condo. But it's time for a change."

Crap. They were serious. How the hell would it all work?

But it was a moot point.

"I'm flattered. Really, I am. But I need to stay in DC for the close proximity to my mom and brother."

At the mention of my brother, my mood tanked. "Speaking of which, do we have any news about Booker?" I asked hopefully.

Cruz nodded slowly. "We have made progress and are feeling pretty good. But for your own safety, we don't want to share any details yet. While we didn't start the mission with the objective of protecting you, it quickly became apparent we needed to do just that. We aren't stopping until both your brother and you are safe."

Well, shit. Now I had a damn lump in my throat. "Th… thank you. I don't know how Booker or I will ever make this up to you. It's probably not even possible," I said with a sniffle.

I left the guys to clean up the mess I'd made in the kitchen and walked down to the dock I'd visited the day before with Thorn. When I was sure no one was around, I called Sunday.

"Hey," she said when she answered. "How much longer do you plan on being out there on the Eastern Shore?"

"I wish I knew. They still don't know where my brother is, as far as I can tell. I just want to get him back so we can all go back to living normally."

"Oh, Joss. This is just so horrible, this whole thing. I'm still staying at my parents'."

My stomach churned with guilt over Sunday having to leave the apartment. I wished she hadn't been affected by this whole mess.

"I'll make this up to you, Sunday. I just feel terrible about everything."

She sighed. "Look, the important thing is to find your brother. What can I do to help, if anything?"

That was a good question. *Could* Sunday be of some sort of help?

MY NEXT CALL was to Candice, which I was dreading. But it had to be done.

"Hello, Joss," she said in a friendly tone.

I was so surprised, I thought I had the wrong person for a moment.

"Candice. I have a few things going on in my life. Family issues. I need to be off work a while longer. I'm very sorry."

"Oh, Joss, everything will be fine. Don't worry, I've got you covered," she said sweetly.

What the hell was going on? Who took Candice, my bitchy boss, and what did they do with her?

"Say, are you at your mother's house?"

Her innocuous question sent a shiver down my spine. Why was she asking? She'd never cared about such things before. In fact, how did she even know my mother lived locally? I never talked about personal things with her unless she was looking for info about my brother.

"Um, no, not at the moment. But you know what, Candice, I need to run. Thank you for understanding!"

I ended the call. Why was she being so nice? And inquisitive?

Because Candice, at least the one I knew, for whom I worked at the Georgetown Library, was neither nice, nor inquisitive.

And now I was re-thinking the last day I'd been at work when I'd found that mysterious note.

Hadn't that come off a rack of books Candice had specifically given me, and even though she knew I didn't feel well, had asked me to stay to shelve?

Holy shit. Did she have something to do with all this? And was that why she was always asking about my brother and flirting with him?

And what about the guy I'd seen leaving the library, looking back at me over his shoulder? What had he looked like, again?

I ran back up to the house and grabbed my sketch pad. As crappy as I was at drawing, I knew if I got down the basics of what I remembered I might have something to share with the Arrow, Cruz, and Thorn. That, coupled with the fact that I suspected Candice was up to no good, made me feel like I was actually doing something.

25

CRUZ DUFRESNE

"Holy crap, Joss. You drew this?"

She shrugged modestly. "Thanks Cruz, but I know it's not that good. I just wanted to see what I could get down on paper."

Arrow peered over my shoulder. "Jesus. That's good. I think we know that guy."

She wrinkled her nose. "Really? I wasn't even sure the drawing looked like a human being, never mind someone you might actually recognize."

I pulled her onto my lap and buried my nose in her hair. I couldn't help myself. "It's rough, for sure, but shit, there's enough here to see where you were going with it."

She shimmied her shoulders a little. "Cool. I guess my little Masterclass is paying off."

Thorn joined us from outdoors, and Arrow waved him over. "Who's this?" he asked, frowning at the sketch.

His eyes widened after he looked a moment longer. "Jesus. Is that Grant Simmons? Did you draw this, Joss?"

She tilted her head toward him. "I tried," she laughed.

"Well, considering we can make out who you were going for, that's pretty fucking awesome." He high-fived Joss. "I think our girl has a future in fine art."

"Yeah, right," she said, play-slapping him. "So, who is this guy, Grant Simmons? Why was he at the Georgetown Library leaving me a note?"

Arrow sat back in the large club chair he always claimed. "Simmons used to work with us. He left The Company a while back. I thought he'd retired to some Caribbean island or something. But it appears he's back in town, and sounds like he's working for the other side now."

Thorn put his head in his hands. "That's what's so fucked about all this. Some of the guys flock to the highest bidder. We're highly trained, and the other side knows that. They'll pay anything to pull us over."

"Does this happen a lot? People going to work for the other side?" Joss asked.

"No, thank god. Most of us have some scruples. Maybe not a lot, but some," Thorn added. "Guess Simmons isn't one of them. Christ, I'd always thought he was a good guy. Booker did too. That's probably how they got him. He most likely thought he could trust Simmons and had no idea he'd gone over."

"Okay, then, what does this mean for my brother?" Joss asked, grinding her little ass on my hard-on.

Arrow laughed when he saw me struggling to speak. What could I say? There was a hot woman sitting on me.

And I was digging it.

"We might be able to track him down through some contacts. Find out a little about what the hell he's up to," Arrow said.

"Well, we know he wants the satchel, and whatever is in it," Thorn said.

I shot him a look to remind him to keep mum about the thumb drive for Joss's safety.

He nodded discreetly. "Whatever's in the satchel probably contained all the evidence Booker had collected about him and his cronies. He knows if that gets into the wrong hands, they're all as good as dead."

Props to Booker for so successfully hiding the intelligence he'd gathered. If he hadn't, and ended up with no leverage over the other side, he'd be a dead man already. Our hanging on to that thumb drive was the only thing keeping him alive. We had to find Simmons and dangle the thumb drive over his head, and we had to do it fast.

The guys and I looked at each other, most likely thinking the same thing. We'd been through this before. But we weren't about to hash it out in front of Joss, not only for her own safety but also to keep her from freaking out. If she knew her brother was so close to being completely fucked, well, that could get ugly. We didn't need her going rogue again.

I knew she wanted her brother back at any cost, and I didn't blame her. He was a good guy. I had mountains of admiration for him. He'd always been a brilliant soldier and operative. I didn't really understand why he didn't retire when the rest of us did, but it was good for The Company that he hadn't. There weren't many men like him.

"Let's track him down, and try to pass off the fake satchel as the real one," Thorn said.

Joss looked between us all. "Wait. You have a fake satchel?"

Arrow nodded. "Yup. And we may need your help delivering it."

"Anything I can do," she said eagerly.

I could think of a few things she could do to help us out right now, and I saw Thorn was thinking the same thing.

"You want to help us, baby?" Thorn asked, looking her up and down. "Then why don't you come over here and help me with this hard-on of mine?"

Bastard. He'd totally just cock-blocked me.

But it was all good. We weren't going to be stingy with our girl.

Joss looked at me. "You mind, Cruz?"

I held my arms up as she got off my lap. "Have at it, baby. Show us how you can help."

With a giggle, Joss sauntered across the living room

and made her way to Thorn who, of course, was wearing a big, shit-eating grin as he removed his classes.

She put her hands on either side of the chair where he sat, and bent over to kiss him, giving Arrow and me a perfect view of her thong-covered ass, made visible by the little skirt she was wearing.

Holy shit, this woman was fucking hot.

She ground her ass in our direction and Thorn reached for her tits as they tongued each other.

"Pull that thong down, baby," Arrow demanded, adjusting himself in his jeans.

Seemed we all had hard dicks. There was a lot of that going around lately.

She glanced over her shoulder. Smiling, she reached under her skirt and slipped the thong below her ass and down to her ankles. She kicked it aside and bent over again to get back to kissing Thorn.

And what a show she was giving us. Her smooth, bare pussy glistened with her juices and her asshole was puckered and pink.

Yeah, the one I'd fucked just the day before. I couldn't wait to get back in there. But I was a patient man.

Arrow looked at me and smiled. "You ever see anything so pretty?" he asked.

I shook my head. "Certainly not."

And it was true.

Joss, like the champ that she was, worked her way down to Thorn's jeans, which she opened in a long, slow, torturous movement.

It was agonizing to watch, and it must have been that much more so for Thorn.

When her hand was full with his erection, she gave us all a smile with one more look over her shoulder, and lowered her mouth over his hard-on.

His head fell back and he closed his eyes with a groan as she deep-throated him in one quick movement.

Never one to miss out on the action, Arrow got up and positioned himself behind Joss. He placed a pillow under her knees where she knelt in front of Thorn, which raised her ass several inches. Then he buried his face between her cheeks and even with her mouth full, she managed to shriek with pleasure.

Did I feel left out? Fuck no. It was goddamn hot watching my friends work over this beautiful woman. In fact, it was so hot, I pulled my own dick out of my pants and began stroking it.

From where I sat, I saw Arrow put one finger in Joss's pussy, and his thumb in her ass. She ground back against him like she had when I'd filled her with my dick, and the more excited she got, the more enthusiasm she visited on Thorn's cock.

With an ear-splitting bellow, Thorn pushed Joss's head down and bucked his hips while he squeezed his eyes shut. The cords on his neck strained and he shuddered, presumably filling her mouth with cum.

She released him and pushed back against Arrow's invading fingers, her own moans increasing as he pumped her harder.

"Oh god," she wailed. "Yes, fuck me like that."

Thorn smiled down at her while she bucked under Arrow's ministrations. An orgasm hit her hard and when it was over, she collapsed with her head in Thorn's lap.

He gestured in my direction. "Baby, I think Cruz has a little something for you."

She raised her head slowly, wearing a drunk smile, her eyes half closed. "Whatcha got?" she whispered.

"Why don't you come over here and find out?" I said, continuing to stroke myself.

Arrow helped her up and she wobbled in my direction.

"Either of you guys got a condom?" I asked.

"Yo," Thorn said, pulling one out of his pocket and tossing it my way.

"C'mon, baby," I said while I sheathed myself. "Straddle daddy's lap here."

She hiked her skirt to her waist, and with her hands on my shoulders, hovered her pussy right over my dick.

"Are you ready, baby?" I asked, holding my rigid dick.

She nodded weakly. "Always ready," she murmured.

I parked myself at her opening while Arrow and Thorn watched with big smiles. With my hand on her hip, I lowered her until she was completely impaled.

She gave a little cry when I drew her down hard, knowing that my dick was stretching her wide open. A moment later, her head dropped back, she put her hands behind my neck, and she began to ride me like she was possessed.

I knew I couldn't hold my cum, so I put a thumb on

her clit to make sure she got off first. Arrow had walked up behind her and with her head tilted back, put several fingers in her mouth.

What a fucking sight. What was I going to do with this woman?

Or, rather, what was I going to do without her?

I had to get her to come back to my ranch. There, she could draw all day long, and not have to worry about a low-paying job in DC.

I'd have her do other things all day long, too, because she was one woman I wanted to keep very happy.

∧

26

JOSS PEYTON

"Good news, guys. Just made contact through an intermediary with Simmons."

What? What had Thorn just said?

I ran into Arrow's room where the guys were chatting. "What? What's going on? What did you just say, Thorn?"

The three of them turned toward me, and if I wasn't mistaken, *oh shit* was written across their faces.

What the hell?

"Oh, um, well…" Thorn started to say but petered off.

Jesus. These guys called themselves professionals? They were never going to find my brother at this rate.

Thank god I'd enlisted Sunday's help. I could trust her.

Between the two of us, we'd get to the bottom of things, including whether or not my psycho boss knew anything.

Arrow took a deep breath. "Joss, Thorn was just saying that… we've tracked down the guy you saw in the library, Simmons."

Okay. That was progress.

"Excellent. Now, how long till we find my brother?"

More silence.

I put my hands on my hips, ready to let them have it. I didn't care if I'd just had sex with all three of them. I had my priorities.

Thorn held his hands up in surrender. "Guys, we need to tell Joss what's going on."

There was stuff they weren't telling me? What the fuck.

"Um, yeah. What are you guys holding back? Because this is bullshit. My brother wouldn't have brought me into this if he didn't think I could be trusted."

Cruz nodded slowly. "Joss, we found a thumb drive hidden in the shoulder strap of your brother's bag—"

"That's amazing! What's on it?" I burst out.

He shook his head. "It's encrypted and Thorn hasn't been able to get into it. But that almost doesn't matter. What does, is that we know someone wants it, and to what extent they'll go to get it back. This gives us leverage in negotiating for your brother."

"We have a meeting point set up in Georgetown down by the old C&O Canal. You will bring a decoy bag in exchange for Booker."

My stomach flipped. "Me?" I said in a small voice.

Thorn gave me a tiny smile. "Yeah. I actually set it up using your phone. Didn't think you'd mind if it meant Booker's safe return. The folks on the other end think they were corresponding with you."

"Okay. I'll just give them the decoy bag and they'll free Booker. Right?"

Once again, the guys just looked at each other.

"It… may not be quite that easy, Joss," Arrow said.

Of course not. Why did I even think that for a second?

Because I was an idiot, that's why.

Or maybe because I was a library assistant and not a goddamn lethally-trained spy?

"Are we… I mean, am I… in danger?" I stammered.

Arrow looked right at me. "You know you are. You don't even need to ask that."

Cruz threw him a dirty look. "But Joss, we are here to protect you. Our job is to minimize any danger."

I steadied my voice. No need to let the guys know I was scared shitless. "Fine. I'll go pack my stuff right now. Let's go."

I ran to my room and slammed the door, confused to the point where it was not only hard to think, but also breathe. I lay on my bed for a few moments, trying to calm myself, thinking of everything that needed to be done.

Sunday was on her way down here, and now she'd miss us. Shit, had I put her in danger by telling her too much?

I stormed back to Arrow's room where the guys were talking quietly. Guess they didn't want me to overhear any more of their grand plans.

"May I have my phone back?" I said, holding my hand out to Thorn.

He reached into his front jeans' pocket. "Sure. Here you go."

I stormed back to my room to call Sunday.

"Hey, girl. Change of plans," I whispered.

"What? Joss? Why are you whispering?"

I put my ear to the door to make sure the guys were still talking. "I don't want the guys to hear. We're heading back to DC right now."

"But I'm already halfway to you. Just stall. Wait for me there."

Ugh. She didn't understand what I was dealing with. "I can't. We don't want them to know I've told you anything. That would be a disaster."

"Right. Okay, you're totally right."

"I'll keep you posted but don't text me yet. They're using my phone to communicate with the people who have Booker. And Sunday, I think my boss might have something to do with all this. Last time I called she was super nice about my being out, and asked *again* how my brother was."

"Oh god, she's such a psycho. I wouldn't put it past her. You know, people say DC is full of spies."

"It's hard to imagine Candice a spy. But why not, you know what I mean?"

She let out a long sigh. "Crazy shit. So, I'll see you in DC, then."

"Thanks Sunday. You're the best."

She laughed. "You too, honey."

As soon as we finished our call, I began to shove all my things back into the duffel I'd brought with me.

Cripes, I'd been in a rush to get out of the hotel, and now was in a rush to get out of here. This bullshit had better be over soon because the stress was going to send me to an early grave.

I flung my door open to find the guys already prepared to go. Jesus, they were fast.

"Do we need to clean up or anything?" I asked, taking one last look around the house.

Under different circumstances, I would have loved to enjoy the place for longer. But duty called.

"No. There's a cleaning service. Let's go," Arrow said, holding the door for me.

It turned out the guys had already thought through all the details of the handoff that was supposed to take place for my brother. They just hadn't bothered to share much of it with me.

"How will all this work?" I asked.

"You will walk to the designated hand-off location with your brother's bag. We will be watching, all from different vantage points so we can help if and when needed."

Thorn, next to me in the backseat, took my hand. "You

won't be alone. We'll be right there, and you'll be perfectly safe."

Easy for him to say.

Jesus. Shit was getting real. And I was scared to death I'd put Sunday in danger. Why hadn't I kept my big mouth shut, and just conducted my own investigation?

I would have just given the damn bag to whatever creeps wanted it, gotten my brother back, and everything would be fine.

Now we were going to fuck around with decoy bags, drop-off points, stake-out locations, and a bunch of other bullshit. If these guys were pros, why was everything so complicated?

And what was up with them wanting to date me? In what imaginary world did three guys date the same woman—especially when they were friends with her brother?

On the other hand, maybe Booker wouldn't object I mean, if he cared about these guys the way they seemed to care about him, might he approve?

But it didn't matter. I wasn't leaving DC, and none of those guys were moving there.

So that was that.

Even though they were gorgeous. And we had amazing sex. And they believed in me and supported me.

Just then a text came through on my phone.

getting close?

Shit, I'd told Sunday not to text me.

"What was that?" Thorn asked.

I hit *delete* and shoved my phone back in my pocket. "Oh nothing. Just one of those weird weather updates."

He looked at me for a moment then smiled. "Oh, I get those, too."

I leaned my head back on the seat, wishing I could doze even if only for a few minutes to grab a little break from my worries. But just when I needed it most, sleep shunned me, leaving me to stew in anxiety about pretty much every aspect of my life.

How did an ordinary library assistant get into such a goddamn mess?

27

THORN JENSEN

"Don't worry Joss, everything will be okay."

"Thanks, Thorn."

She looked at me forlornly, slammed the car door, and began walking down Wisconsin Avenue head down, hands stuffed in her pocket, wearing the satchel across her chest. She looked like any other young woman out for a morning walk.

No one looking at her would ever know the danger she was facing. And how freaking brave she was being.

But she wanted her brother back. Shit, we all did.

I watched her get smaller in the rear-view mirror while Arrow navigated toward the Georgetown waterfront, where we'd leave the SUV and assume each of our watch positions for the satchel drop-off.

Cruz quickly pulled on his homeless man disguise, complete with dirt all over his exposed skin and a wig that looked like a rat's nest.

He brought his wrist up to his mouth as he walked away. "Testing, testing."

We did the same with the radios we were wearing. "All good, Cruz."

He waved over his shoulder and began to walk toward the old canal.

Arrow zipped the gym bag carrying a variety of weapons and headed out toward the fire escape we'd scouted for him to watch from.

I headed a few blocks in the opposite direction until I found an address I was given by one of our intermediaries. I pressed the code on the side of the garage and the door opened with a creak. Inside I found the Yamaha FZ1 bike I'd requested with a helmet on the seat and the key in the ignition. I let the bike warm up for a minute and peeled out to take my station for the hand off.

It felt good to be on a bike again. I had one at home in San Francisco but hardly ever used it, that's how busy I was with my cyber work.

It had been nice to get away from that grind for a while. I'd forgotten how satisfying it was to be on a mission and even more so when we were helping a friend.

But the best part of this gig had been meeting Joss. What a cool girl. Gorgeous, smart, sexy, ballsy—she was the complete package as far as I was concerned. I didn't think it was too likely we'd see much of her after our current job wrapped up, but one could always hope.

I idled the bike a block away from where I could now see Joss hanging out, sitting on a bench by the old canal and pretending to read a book. She occasionally turned a page and when she did, would discreetly glance around for any sign of action.

Yeah, she wasn't reading a single word on those pages. No way she could concentrate.

We guys had to be super careful, because of course the other side—whoever the hell they were—probably also had people watching the hand-off. That's why I pretended to tinker with my bike's engine, and Cruz was wandering around digging in trash cans. I couldn't see Arrow, who was tucked away out of sight, ready to pounce.

I casually pulled my wrist up. "Everyone all set?" I asked.

"Roger that," echoed in my earpiece.

I continued tinkering while a slow-moving van idled on a corner. Joss saw it too, and casually turned another page in her book.

The van started moving and crept up the block toward her.

It was them. Definitely them.

C'mon Joss, I chanted to myself. You can do this.

But when does anything in life go according to plan?

Joss was supposed to approach the van to make sure

Booker was in it. Instead, she froze. The van door slid open and a woman had leaned out.

"Sunday!" Joss exclaimed.

Sunday? Wasn't that her friend? Or her roommate?

What the fuck?

Confusion all over her face, Joss got up and slowly walked toward the van. "Sunday? Are you okay?" she asked.

"Help me, Joss, help me!" she screamed, leaning out of the van.

No, Joss, don't.

But at the sight of her friend crying for help, Joss took the outstretched hand. Before she could react, she was yanked inside. The door slammed and the van took off.

Fuck.

I was already back on the bike and swung by Cruz, who hopped on the back in his homeless duds.

"What the fuck was that?" he said over the engine's roar.

"Isn't Sunday her roommate?"

"Yeah. Her fucking roommate was in on this whole thing?" he shouted.

We followed the speeding van down the Rockcreek Parkway as it clumsily wove in and out of heavy DC traffic. It was no match for the agile motorcycle we were on, and we quickly caught up.

I pulled up next to the van to get a look at the driver, but when he looked our way, I hit the brakes and dropped back.

"Do you think they know we're on their tail?" Cruz asked.

"I sure as hell hope not."

It was surprising they'd used the clichéd van to grab Joss. They were pretty much impossible to hide, and were slow and difficult to maneuver. I expected the folks who'd taken Booker to have a more sophisticated operation.

But maybe these were amateurs? Who the fuck knew?

And what would they do when they found out the bag Joss had was just a decoy? This wasn't good.

In fact, it was pretty fucking bad.

But they weren't going to get away with it. No fucking way.

28

JOSS PEYTON

"Shut up, Joss. I'm warning you. Shut up."

Sunday—my roommate and supposed friend—was holding a gun.

And pointing it straight at me.

I closed my eyes and swallowed as the van careened around a curve in the road. Because the windows were blacked out, I wasn't positive where we were going. But since we were clearly on a twisty road, my best guess was that it was the Rockcreek Parkway. The question was, were we heading north or south?

And even if I knew, would it make any difference?

Before it had sunk in that Sunday had a gun pointed at

me, I'd responded to her cry for help. What else was I going to do for her? Of course, I wanted to help.

When she first pulled me in the van, I sprawled on the floor and started sliding around when the driver hit the gas. I reached out to Sunday for help, but just looked at my outstretched hand like she had no idea what I wanted.

"Sunday, help me!" I yelled, rolling in the other direction as the van swerved.

She rolled her eyes and helped me into a seat.

"Oh my god, Sunday, they got you too. I'm so sorry. I never should have dragged you into this mess."

The guilt was overwhelming. She didn't deserve to get sucked into my brother's drama.

She just kept looking at me with a gaze I didn't recognize.

"Sweetie, are you okay?" I asked. "Did they hurt you? Talk to me."

But when I reached out to touch her arm, she slapped my hand away.

Oh my god. What had they done to her?

And what were they going to do to me?

"Give me the bag," she hissed, pointing at the satchel crossing my chest.

I shook my head. "No, Sunday. This is for the people holding Booker hostage."

She put her head in her hand for a moment then snapped back up at me. "For fuck's sake, Joss, give me the bag."

The look in her eyes was so cold it made me shiver.

"Sunday, I... I don't understand."

"Joss, who the fuck do you think I am?" she barked.

Okay, things were getting officially weird.

"Wh... what do you mean?" I stammered.

She smacked her hand on the seat and hollered to whoever was driving. "Can you believe this shit?" she hollered at him. "She still has no idea what's going on."

She was right. I didn't. In fact, I was so confused, coupled with the motion of the van, I was getting dizzy.

That's all I needed, to barf or pass out.

That's when I leaned my head back on my car seat and closed my eyes.

"Sunday, would you please tell me what the hell—"

When she screamed for me to shut up, I sat up and looked at her.

That's when I saw she'd pulled a gun on me.

"You dumb fuck, Joss. Did you really think we were friends? Did you really think I wanted to hang out with someone like you?"

Had someone just punched me in the stomach? Because it sure felt like it.

"But... but..." I stumbled.

"Shut up and give me the goddamn bag before I pull it off you," she screamed.

"Why? Sunday, are you working for the people who took my brother?" My eyes started to fill with tears.

Dammit. The last thing I wanted to do was cry right then.

Shaking her head, she narrowed her eyes. I never dreamed I'd be afraid of Sunday, but now I was terrified.

"Of course I do, you dumb fuck. He interfered in our operations."

"But you were always so nice to him. I thought you liked him."

She dropped her head back to cackle. "Of course I was nice to him. I was trying to fuck him to get information when he started getting too close to figuring out who I was. So, we had to grab him."

Holding back the tears didn't work, and a couple fat ones dribbled down my cheeks.

"All those nights you were away—were they really booty calls?" I asked, afraid I already knew the answer.

She rolled her eyes again. "Of course not. I was working those nights. Fucking a bunch of guys was just my cover."

Oh. My. God. I had been completely and totally duped. What a fucking idiot I was.

But how was I to know my roommate was a freaking spy or whatever the hell she was?

"So you befriended me just to fuck me over, huh?" I asked, my growing rage bubbling just below the surface. "And your people took my brother?"

I wanted to smack the smug right off her face. But that could wait. I had to think carefully to find a way through my fucked up situation.

"Now are you going to give me the bag or do I have to take it from you?" she asked.

The van suddenly stopped.

I just looked at her.

"Look, either way, you and your brother are going to be dead soon. So I'll leave it up to you. I can take it now, or after your brains have been blown out."

Fuck me. If she didn't have that gun in her hand, I'd tear her eyes out with my bare fingers.

Now I was really pissed.

But I didn't let on.

I was going to find a way to *fuck this bitch up*.

Even if I died doing it.

"What about my boss at the library? Is she in on this too?"

The van door slid open, and Sunday pushed me toward it. "Of course not. That idiot? I'm surprised she can even read."

Wow. I'd been on the wrong track.

I looked around the parking garage we'd entered while Sunday pulled me toward a nondescript white door.

"We're in the Kennedy Center parking garage, if you can't tell. C'mon. There are tunnels and safe rooms in case the president or other dignitaries are here and there's a terrorist attack."

Wow. I had no idea.

The heavy door slammed behind us but not before I looked back to see if the guys had managed to follow us. Seeing no one, my heart sank.

Fuck. They'd never find me here.

But that suddenly didn't matter. At the end of a maze of long hallways, we entered a room that held my brother.

29

ARROW SULLIVAN

I CAME TO A HARD STOP IN FRONT OF THE KENNEDY Center, after Thorn had let me know he and Cruz had managed to get into the building's parking garage. I was grateful to find that all its theaters were dark for the night.

Less collateral damage that way.

And it also explained how Thorn and Cruz had almost gotten shut out of the parking garage.

The people we were up against obviously had some sort of 'in' at the Kennedy Center. As their van had approached, Thorn told me the metal gates on the garage lifted, and he and Cruz had slipped in on the bike, unnoticed, just before it closed.

Armed with this information, I headed straight for the front drive and ran around the side to the staff door. Fortunately for me, some musician was just on his way out, presumably after practice, and I slipped in and headed for the garage.

"What level are you guys on?" I asked through the radio.

"Level two," Cruz answered quietly. "It looks like the van went down to level three, but we are waiting for you here."

"On my way," I said, running down the steep escalators to the garage.

Thank god there were no shows scheduled for that evening.

When I reached the guys, we continued on foot, silently making our way to the garage's lower level.

As soon as we rounded a corner, we found the van, parked haphazardly, with the doors left open.

There was no sign of life.

They must have known we were close on their trail.

We ran across the garage with our weapons drawn, and confirmed it was empty.

"Hey, guys," Cruz said, "they parked really close to this door right here. Do you think that's maybe where they were going?"

It was worth trying.

I pulled a couple pins out of my pocket and got the door unlocked in moments. We entered a long hallway and let the door close silently behind us.

"Shit, it's like a maze down here. This is where all their HVAC stuff is, but have you guys ever heard there's also a safe room in case the president or someone needs it?"

"No shit?" Thorn said. "I never knew that. You think that's where they are?"

I glanced at him. "Your guess is as good as mine."

We rounded a corner and for the first time, heard voices in the distance.

I sure as hell hoped it was Joss and Booker.

"This is *not* the right satchel!" a woman's voice screamed.

Sunday?

"It's the only one I had," Joss lied. "Booker, tell them this is your satchel."

"It sure looks like it," he said quietly.

Which was a good move on his part. He knew how we were approaching this mission.

"Where's the drive with our information, Booker?" a male voice asked. "I'm tired of asking you this. I want it now."

I heard the click of a gun.

Cruz and Thorn each took one side of the closed door, and I took the lead. I shoved the door open and we rushed in. Joss, standing next to her bruised brother, flinched at the commotion and threw her arms around him.

The kidnappers, distracted, momentarily turned their attention from their prisoners. Booker took the opportunity to lunge for the guy holding a gun on him, and Cruz tackled the woman.

Someone's gun discharged and Joss screamed.

When I realized we'd secured the weapons of Sunday and her accomplice, I found that she'd been hit in the lower leg. I wasn't sure whose bullet had gotten her, but was happy she wasn't mortally wounded, but rather just in a huge deal of pain.

Joss took a step toward her, but I waved her back.

"No, Joss."

She looked at Sunday with deep pain in her eyes. "I can't believe… that you are behind this. You rotten liar. You pretended to be my friend."

Sunday, rolling around the floor, holding her leg in agony, hissed back. "Go fuck yourself, both you and your brother."

I guess that was about all Joss could take because, before anyone could stop her, she'd gotten a running start and kicked Sunday as hard as she could in her injured leg.

I had a feeling the screams were heard all the way back to Georgetown.

Joss ran to her brother and began to sob. "I… was… afraid I'd never see you again," she stammered.

He held her while looking at us guys, thanking each of us with just a look.

That's how we guys rolled.

BACK AT THE HOTEL, where we waited to do a debrief with some of Booker's fellow operatives.

In the meantime, I ordered a shitload of food from room service. Booker was looking a little thin.

"Did you know you were holed up in the freaking Kennedy Center basement?" Thorn asked. "That's so crazy. Of all places."

Fresh out of the shower, Booker took a swig of his beer. "I had no idea. I was blindfolded when they brought me in. I could have been in bumfuck anywhere, for all I knew."

Joss shook her head in disbelief. "It is kind of funny you were in the Kennedy Center. Think of all the concerts we've seen there over the years. Who knew," she said.

I took a seat on one of the hotel suite's sofas next to Joss and put my arm around her shoulder. Poor thing was still shaking.

"You gonna be okay?" I asked her quietly.

She nodded and looked nervously in the direction of her brother.

Who hadn't batted an eye.

There was a knock on the door. Booker got up to answer it, and he and two men from The Company retreated to one of the bedrooms to speak in private.

"I can't believe my roommate was in on this whole thing. That fucking bitch."

That's the Joss I knew. She didn't take anything sitting down.

"I should have kicked her ass after you guys got her gun. I'd show her who to fuck with."

Cruz chuckled. "Jesus. Look at the big balls on Joss."

She shot him a look. "Not balls. *Ovaries*."

We burst out laughing.

"So look, Joss. The mission is over. That means it's time to talk about next steps," I said.

She looked up at me. "What do you mean, next steps?"

Cruz took a seat on the club chair across from us while Thorn let room service in with our food.

"Sweetie, we can't live in the Mayflower Hotel forever. We've all got to get back home," Cruz said.

She looked down and nodded sadly.

"But that doesn't mean we can't all be together," he added.

"I… I know you guys mentioned about… being together. I just don't see how that would work."

Cruz settled back in his chair. "Look at it this way, Joss. Do you want to be a library assistant forever?"

She laughed. "Of course not."

"What we were thinking," he said, looking at Thorn and me, "was that we all go back to the ranch for a while to chill out. We're thinking about going back into service and… well, we'd love to have you by our side."

Joss rolled her eyes. "Yeah, I'm really useful. I only got myself kidnapped and nearly killed today."

"If you hadn't been brave enough to do that, we might not have your brother here with us right now," I said.

"We're not talking about going back in with The Company," Thorn said. "We're thinking of doing our own thing. Team up with us and use that international relations degree of yours."

She broke into a huge smile after a deep breath. "Okay. I'll do it. But only with my brother's blessing. I want to be with you guys, too. I have all along, and was afraid to hope you felt the same."

∧

AFTER A PERFUNCTORY INTERVIEW with each of us, The Company took off and we dove into what were the best freaking burgers we'd ever tasted. Of course, everything was enhanced thanks to the excitement of having Booker back in one piece and knowing Joss was game for our proposal.

I'd ordered a couple bottles of champagne to celebrate with, and I poured everyone a glass.

"It feels good for all of us to be together again. Damn, it's been a long time," I said, raising my glass.

Was I getting a lump in my throat?

I didn't do shit like that.

"I… don't know how I can ever thank you guys for getting my ass out of that bad situation," Booker said. "But I especially want to thank my little sister for being such a brave and badass woman."

Everyone raised their glasses and *cheers* erupted around the room.

"Booker, since you're here, there's a favor I'd like to ask of you. Actually, we'd all like to ask it of you."

"What's that?" he asked, eyebrows raised, looking around the room.

"We… are all interested in dating your sister. We plan to bring her back to Cruz's ranch while we have a little R&R, and we'd like your blessing."

He set his champagne glass down and sat back in his chair, slowly crossing his arms. I glanced at Joss, who was nearly shaking.

Shit. This wasn't looking good.

He frowned at Joss. "You want to date these clowns?" he asked, gesturing at the three of us.

She took a deep breath and with her chin held high, sat up straight in her chair. "Yes, I do. I know I don't need your approval. But it would be nice to have."

He scowled at all of us, then picked his champagne glass up and took a sip.

His face slowly turned pink, then red. What the fuck? Was he having a heart attack?

And he burst out laughing, slapping his knee and pointing at each of us.

"You assholes," he said. "Of course you can date my sister if she's crazy enough to want you."

He rolled with laughter as we all looked at each other and finally joined him.

Joss jumped off the sofa and ran to throw her arms around him.

When we'd finally calmed down and Joss had kissed and hugged the guys and me, Cruz pulled her into his lap.

"I don't know how this business of dating all these guys works Joss, but more power to you," Booker said.

She smiled beautifully. "I'm not sure I know how it works either. But we sure as hell will figure it out."

∧

EPILOGUE

I was learning to ride horses.

Yup. Me. The city girl was on her way to being bona-fide country. Cruz had even bought me cowboy boots. They killed my feet at first, but after they were broken in, they were more comfortable than my Converse Chucks. No wonder everyone in Montana wore them day and night.

But I hadn't gone completely country even if I was wearing boots more than sneakers. I still kept my hair dyed nearly black, and wore bright red lipstick every chance I got. Yeah, it got me some weird looks on the ranch and in town, but I didn't care.

My brother had taken to ranch life like a duck to water. He'd always been like that, adaptable to whatever situation he found himself in. I suspect that was part of his training with The Company, but I didn't ask. I figured the less I knew about that shit, the better.

After he'd recovered from his latest ordeal, he rented out his DC apartment and headed to the ranch for an indefinite period of time. He needed to relax and regroup, although I had a feeling his visit might become a bit more long-term than he'd initially planned.

It was amazing to have a chunk of time to spend with him, something that hadn't happened since we were kids. He was finally joining Arrow, Cruz, and Thorn in retiring from The Company. No number of missions would avenge my father's death and if anything, each one he accepted brought him closer to the end of his own life. So, he was done with all that shit, at least that's what he claimed. The guys were forming their own organization now, and I had a feeling my brother wouldn't be able to say no.

Last I heard about Sunday—real name Sasha Yahontov—was that she was on her way to a nice, long stint in Federal prison. I'd not seen or heard from her since the Kennedy Center garage battle, when she was carted away in an ambulance, handcuffed of course, screaming and swearing a blue streak.

After some people from The Company went through the stuff she'd left behind in the apartment, I'd sold what was left on Craigslist and made a hundred bucks or so. I just wanted any reminder of her gone from my life.

I'd also sold most of my own crap with the exception of the tattered sitting chair I'd swiped from my brother so long ago and lovingly dragged around from one living situation to another. I was just too attached to it, and the guys were happy to have it shipped to the ranch, where it could comfortably live out the rest of its days until it completely disintegrated.

Candice actually seemed a little bummed when I told her I was leaving the library and moving to Montana. She told me she'd never had such a hard-working employee. I nearly fell over. I attributed her strange niceness to the fact that she'd landed a new guy—a patron of the library, of course—and was at last getting laid.

Then, there were the guys. My guys. My loves. They'd all taken rooms in the ranch's main house, and I got the guest cottage, which I'd lobbied for in the interest of having some personal space. But I rarely ever spent a night there alone. I just couldn't resist the company of my hot soldiers.

Arrow hadn't completely given up his life in New York, just like Thorn hadn't given up his in San Francisco. It looked like both of them were going to be commuters to the ranch, although as time wore on, they spent more and more time in Montana, and less in their old homes. Ranch life was something people had to ease into.

But it was nice to have options.

Like which guy—or guys—I might hang out with on any given day. We just went with the flow, and it was beautiful. We had as much together and alone time as we wanted. I couldn't be happier, and I was pretty sure I could say the same for them.

We were still learning, but we were doing it as a family, and that was all we really needed.

∧

Did you like *Her Dirty Soldiers*? Learn about the next book
in the Men at Work series,
Check out *Her Dirty Builders*

I hope you loved reading this book as much as I loved writing it. Please visit my store to learn more about my books, and to buy directly from me!
https://mikalaneshop.com/

ABOUT THE AUTHOR

Dear Reader:

I'm USA TODAY bestselling romance author Mika Lane, and am OBSESSED with bringing you sassy, steamy stories with imperfect heroines and the bad-a*s dudes they bring to their knees. I'll always bring you my signature humor and heat, topped off with a modern-day happily ever after.

My first book ever was *The Day I Ate the Milkyway*, a true fourth-grade masterpiece illustrated with crayons and bound with construction paper and glue. Nowadays, steamy romance gives purpose to my days and nights as I create worlds and characters that tickle the imagination. I live in magical Northern California with my own handsome alpha dude, sometimes known as Mr. Mika Lane, and two devilish cats named Chuck and Murray.

A dual citizen of the United States and Ireland, I have on more than one occasion spent my last dollar on a plane ticket somewhere, and am always planning my next escape. I often try new recipes on unsuspecting friends, search out hiding places to read undisturbed, and sadly kill every houseplant I bring home.

I LOVE to hear from readers when I'm not dreaming up naughty tales to share. Visit my online shop https://mikalaneshop.com/ and say hello https://mikalaneshop.com/pages/meet-mika.

xoxo, Mika